CARMEN'S Journey

RICHARD MALMED

ISBN
978-1-956161-48-9 (Hardcover)
978-1-956161-47-2 (Paperback)
978-1-956161-46-5 (eBook)

TABLE OF CONTENTS

CHAPTER ONE

Carmen's Journey

"Meester Magen, may I come in?" Roselita, our cleaning lady, in her timid voice, was always afraid to disturb me as I sat at the computer in my office. I had semi-retired from practicing law a few years earlier, and had made one of the bedrooms my kids vacated into my office. Usually Roselita just wanted to empty the waste basket and dust the desk and computer. Today, she came and waited patiently at the door. "Benge aqui, por favor." I made my meager attempt at practicing my Spanish, before I turned around front to face her. When I saw her though, she was obviously distraught. She was a tiny lady from Honduras who had worked for us and many of our friends for years. My wife and her friends had her signed up for four days a week. She and her cousin would come in to help with our big family dinners. She had worked for us and our friends so long that she felt like our personal treasure. Today, her eyes were filled with tears and her chin was actually trembling. Her normally pretty little mayan features were a tragic mask. "Aw, Roselita, what's the matter? Che passa?"

"My niece, she lock up." Now, the tears started to flow as she came up to my desk. Words or rather sounds poured out of her I couldn't understand, little gasps, hiccups. In between blowing her nose and wiping her eyes, she managed a few syllables of indecipherable Spanish. "Your niece. What happened?" Even after years in the US, Roselita's English was limited. As she started to blubber and cry, it was even worse. I got my daughter on the phone and put her on speaker.

Fortunately, I had caught her at a lull in her job. She managed a nonprofit and was the agent of a number of latino musical groups and spoke fluent Spanish and Portuguese.

"Sweet pea (my name for my daughter), Roselita is trying to tell me something about her niece, and I can't understand her. Can you tell what she is talking about?" After several long bursts of Spanish from either side amid much hiccuping and sobbing from Roselita, Sweet Pea was able to make out that Roselita's niece Carmen had been arrested for something that sounded like prostitution and drugs. She was only 16 and was being held at the Juvenile Detention facility because they couldn't find her mother. (Her father had disappeared long ago.) Roselita was the only thing approaching a responsible family member for Carmen, because her mother was an addict and lived with a man who apparently beat her up regularly. Carmen had been a beautiful wonderful child who seemed to be doing well until she became a teenager a few years ago when she had started to hang with the bad guys in the neighborhood. Now, she needed a lawyer to get her out of jail and find out what this was all about.

I had been a lawyer for many years and just recently moved my office back into my house where I continued to handle a few old clients, but mainly I went to the gym, played golf or tried to finish a few of the books I had started to write. As a lawyer, I had usually been a commercial litigator for big companies. That means I tried conflicts involving business matters. But from the early days in my practice on, I did almost everything else. I had long ago been an assistant district attorney and continued to do some criminal law. I was an oddity in my firm because this part of my practice took me into areas few of them even imagined. It was a great chance to get out of the stuffy, self-satisfied world of corporate business.

But each area of law has its own customs, and before you can hope to practice in any of them, you have to know its ways. Criminal law was no exception. It required the least amount of book learning, but the greatest amount of street smarts. You had to know the minor judiciary, the cops, and above all the streets. Normally, a juvenile criminal matter was resolved in the juvenile system with a term of probation and a stern lecture. I thought I could help Roselita's family with a few short court appearances. The juvenile court was the dumping ground for judges not deemed capable of real legal matters. So I went down to the detention facility to hear what

Roselita's niece Carmen could tell me. I arrived just in time to see another shift of juvenile defendants brought up for processing at a preliminary arraignment, that is a bail hearing where they would be released pending trial. After a while, Carmen Jacinto was called up and released on bail into my custody pending a hearing in 10 days in Juvenile Court. I walked up to her as she left the courtroom and introduced myself while explaining that

Roselita had asked me to represent her.

"You ain't no P.D.?" she asked with a haughty smile. She didn't want the public defender.

"No, I'm a private lawyer."

"Well, you got white hair. You been around?"

"Yes I been around. Do you want me or not? If so, let's talk." "Yeah, I guess so, but I'm hungry and I want to go home." "Okay, I'll buy breakfast and we'll talk then. Where's home?" "Well, I ain't gonna my mom's. She's got that bum over. I guess

Tía Roselita."

"Okay, fine. Let's eat."

We went to the Aramingo Diner. An old fashioned steel diner in North Philly which had an all day breakfast menu. I got a booth in the back. The locals from the lower Northeast eyed us—some with amusement, some without curiosity. An older guy in business suit walking with a sexy little teeny with heavy makeup.

Carmen was a very pretty girl, very petit build with huge dark eyes. Her cheeks were stained with the marks of mascara and eye liner she had put on, but had obviously run from all the crying she had been doing. She wore a low cut, bare midriff top in bright pink, with a purple skirt so short and tight she could hardly walk. She wore those high heels with the heavy cork base making her four inches taller. She was putting two huge earrings back on her ears. Half of her head was shaved to reveal a multi-color tattoo of something or other. There were a few more tats on her upper arms. Ominously, there were a number of black and blue marks on her upper arms and thighs.

"I don't owe you nothing for this, do I?"

"No. No. Roselita is taking care of everything." In fact, I was doing this for free for Roselita, who had been a staple in my family life for many years, now and was entitled to a few favors.

Carmen ordered a huge breakfast—ham, eggs, pancakes, toast. "This is on you, too, right?"

"Yes, Carmen. I got it. Eat what you like. Now, tell me first how old you are and then what got you locked up."

"Okay. I'm sixteen, but I never had a quinceañera." She was referring to a big party hispanic girls usually have thrown in their honor. "Tía Roselita's daughter got one, but my mom said she was tapped." She was telling me she had lost prestige in the latino community and was looked down on by those who were respectable and found their way in the U.S.

"Now, what happened?"

"Okay. I'm hanging in Tito's bar talking to this guy when the cops come in and arrest everyone. I'm underage so they lock me up."

"The charges are prostitution and drugs. So they claim you were doing a lot more than that. Remember, I'm your lawyer. Unless I know the facts, I can't help you." As unbelievable as it may seem, almost no criminal client tells you the truth the first time. I call it the Dance of the Seven Veils— they peel off each one as long as the music plays. Maybe they're trying to find a story I'll accept, maybe they don't trust me. Anyway, I have to peel one at a time off.

"They found some coke on the second f loor. Whose coke was it and why were you charged if it was on the second f loor?"

"I don't know whose coke it was, but I go to the second f loor bathroom sometimes. By the way, are they gonna dust those bags for fingerprints?"

"They may. How big were those bags?" (I hadn't said anything about bags, had I? No. And why was she asking about fingerprints? She was working on a better story as we spoke.)

"There were a bundle of dime bags." "How did you see them?"

"The cops brought them down and laid them on the bar." (Good answer. I knew she must have been with them on the second f loor.) "Whoa. A bundle of dime bags. That's a lot, why do they claim you had them?" (This was ten bags which went for between $50 and $100 a bag.)

"I don't know. Cops do strange things." "Was anyone else arrested?"

"Yeah. There was another woman, some tramp."

"Were any of them on the second f loor when the cops came in?" First, a hesitation. Something was going through Carmen's head.

Somehow fitting the story together. "No…I don't know."

"Did you see everyone in the barroom when the cops came in?" "Uh, yes…yes I did."

"Why did they go to the second f loor?" "I don't know. Ask them."

"Was everyone charged with the coke or just you?" "No, just me and this one guy."

"Just you and this guy. What did he look like? Did you know him?" "He was an older guy with dyed black hair. A real small dude a good bit older."

"Do you know his name? Or anything about him?" "No. He's an older guy with a few bucks. Dressed well."

"How do they get this prostitution charge? Did you talk to the cops?"

"No. I know Tio Miranda. I don't talk. Maybe, this guy said something." (Miranda of course was the case which required Miranda warnings and she was claiming criminal street smarts like a seasoned pro.)

"You don't hook? Because they need some fairly strong evidence from the cops or somebody that you were."

"No, I don't hook." She was beginning to shift in her seat, but never missed an opportunity to pack more breakfast away. She was feeling her story slip away and she didn't know what punishment she might face.

While we were talking, Carmen had reached for the hot sauce and sprinkled copious amounts on every morsel on her plate which was not inconsiderable. It hurt my intestines just to look at it. But wolf it down, she did with one hand grabbing a fork and the other the knife. She was done in what seemed like seconds but may have been at least two minutes. "Is there anything you want?"

Carmen eyed the pies on the counter and asked for two slices of Boston Creme Pie. Down it went too. Fortunately without hot sauce. Finally, she looked up at me. She hadn't even made eye contact before, but stared into the table. Now, she looked up with a smirk on her face. "You aren't into young girls, are you. Is that why you took the case?" Street smart and tough. She suspected all men.

She was not that subtle. She knew something always cost something. "No, Carmen. Tía Roselita is a long time friend and I'm doing this for her. You don't owe me anything. But, I got to say your story doesn't hold water. Let me do a little investigating and I'm going to have to go over this again with you. In the meantime, I'll take you to Roselita's." As we got into the car, she was quietly evaluating me. She saw a nice business suit, everything spit and polish like a typical business lawyer. I always wore the right uniform to court—the power suit, shined shoes and always just enough behind the fashion to be respectable but not sharp.

She liked my car. As she walked around to her seat, she was taking inventory. The car was a 2002 Thunderbird, black with a removable hard top. Because it was several years too old, it had the cachet of being fashionably shabby. But latinos and latinas knew their cars. This, in their book, was a rare old classic and spoke well of me. "Nice ride," she said, "but it could use a wax." I was betraying my wonderful ride.

CHAPTER TWO

At Tito's

After dropping Carmen off at Roselita's on a street just off Rising Sun Avenue, I got on the Roosevelt Expressway and began to size up what I had heard. Carmen was too small and young to make it on the street so she had to have some protection, some pimp. All that thin layer of bravado was a bit scary for one so small, especially if she was already doing coke. Something else was afoot. I'd have to see this Tito's Bar where she was hanging out. Who was the john, and who was the pimp. Some kind of cops had raided the bar, but why? If they were really after vice, they could have gone to hundreds of places—the web was full of advertisements—Asians, Russians, older, younger, S + M—take your pick, it was on dozens of different sites for Philly alone. The websites were full of them—Backpage, Escorts, Massages. Why raid this place? Was Carmen working for the house or was she an independent who paid for her protection? Which cops did the raid—the vice cops or the drug cops? Would some cooperation on her part get her off?

I don't know why I ask my clients what their story is. I never get the facts I need from them, in the beginning. Still, Carmen was just a pawn in some larger game. If I knew who else was involved, I could trade her inside information for something—maybe immunity. Of course, I could also plea bargain for probation and walk away, but what if she was charged as an adult and what if the coke was more than just a little bit? She might get some serious time. If she could only tell me who else might be involved, that was the way out. Them that rats first rats best, and I did not want to be left out of the game. I'd stop by Tito's and get the lay of the land.

As I suspected, Tito's was just like hundreds of other corner bars in Philadelphia, but this one was in the hispanic neighborhood. My business suit wouldn't work. I dug into my gym bag and got out my tank top, warm up pants and a warm Underarmor pullover, a beat up leather jacket and a Marlin's baseball cap. Mexicans wore Dodger's hats, Puerto Ricans wore Yankees or Marlin's hats. No Philadelphian would ever wear a Yankee hat. So I went Marlin. I went in the door and a beefy bartender looked up through the afternoon haze.

"You a member?" Ah, he must mean this was a club. Liquor licenses for some reason dating back to Prohibition differentiated between a public tavern and a private club—clubs had longer hours and could exclude non-members (that means cops and any particular disfavored ethnic group).

"No. But I'm working up the street." In Philadelphia, some street's manhole, gas line, sewer line, water line was always under repair. "I just wanted a beer."

"Ok. That'll be five to join and the beer's extra. What's the name?" I guess I had passed the membership test without a blackball. Apparently three references from club members and a credit check were not required.

I could afford the five. I must have passed the bartender's sniff test. "You got Rolling Rock." I said, passing him the five and putting another five on the bar. At these bars, you put your money on the bar and the bartender made change and took the money as the drink was served. Any other transaction would have been viewed with suspicion and my clever disguise would have been blown.

"Yeah, on tap." Wow! Rolling Rock on tap was like going back into a time warp. This was a golden moment. Once, the most popular working man's premium beer in Philly, it had lapsed over the years to the onslaught of that awful Bud monopoly, the lite beers which were beers diluted by water but not by price, and the new yuppy beers. Rolling Rock was my beer of choice ever since we used to go to the blue collar neighborhoods and pay a guy on the corner to buy us a six pack. A distant second was Schmidt's (aka "panther piss") only because it was cheap. Rolling Rock once brewed outside Pittsburgh was now brewed on the west coast. A barroom debate over whether Rolling Rock was the same or ruined could take up an entire evening among the cognoscenti.

Actually, I was a bit surprised the bar was open. If it was raided and arrests were made, it could have been closed on the spot if the bar management was at fault. "So, I hear this place was raided. Any arrests?"

"I hear they arrested a few people for drugs on the second f loor."

"Ok. What's on the second f loor?"

"Just some rooms we rent out for private parties."

After I finished the beer, my bladder began its call. At my age, the bladder has the holding capacity of an eyedropper. But the trip to the men's room let me examine the ceiling of the bar more closely. Sure enough, there was an array of surveillance cameras. Most bar owners had them installed these days to counter light-fingered bartenders. There were dozens of ways bartenders could beat the owner—free drinks for excessive tips, substituting your own bottle, watering to bottles, and the usual— putting the money in the pocket and not the till. I wondered whether the tape covered a 7 or 30 day period. In any case, I relieved myself. The beer had passed through me without changing color. I must have just rented it.

Ok, interesting, but nothing valuable yet. I was thinking about getting something to eat, but I looked behind the bar. Just a hot dog roller and a small stand for salt peanut packages. The minimum food inventory necessary to keep a liquor license. The hot dogs looked like they had been on the roller long enough to substitute for industrial grade rebar for setting concrete. This place was clearly a dump. What was little Carmen doing here? With a little ambition, she could have been a high priced call girl. I finished my beer and left.

I still didn't know what kind of cop conducted the raid. If it was the LCB (Liquor Control Board), they would have shut the place down and needed no warrant to search the place. If it was the vice cops or the narcs, then, someone had to tip them off about something and they needed a warrant.

CHAPTER THREE

$2k Payment

As I got home, I saw a muscle car sitting in my driveway with the engine running. It was a purple Mustang with two wide stripes running lengthwise. I had to park in the street since the car was blocking my driveway. As I walked down the driveway, a small thin latino man with a pencil mustache got out and handed me an envelope. "My boss says this is for Carmen's case. Don't fuck up." He got back in the car and left before I could ask him anything.

The envelope held a thick wad of $20s. I knew this was trouble so I was careful not to touch the envelope in more than one place and not count the bills. It was about $2000. Someone was interested in "protecting" Carmen, but it was more than that. I put the envelope and cash in a baggy and put it in the freezer.

Carmen already knew I was representing her for free at the request of her aunt Roselita. As a lawyer, I then owed a duty of loyalty and confidentiality only to Carmen, not even Roselita. This money from someone unknown could create a conflict of interest. It was designed to have Carmen know that whoever gave me the money was interested in her not giving any information against them. In a way, it was a threat delivered through me. She was to know that someone—whoever it was—was watching her case and wanted her to simply plead guilty, take protection and move on.

I now knew a few things. Carmen was somehow involved with a person who made money from her work, that she knew something valuable about them. However, by showing this supposedly good faith act of paying her lawyer, she was being told that she was still part of "the team" and would be somehow rewarded for her loyalty. It was a frequent practice of the major drug dealers. Every time one of them got arrested, the same lawyers always seemed to represent the junior associates, i.e. street pushers. As a result, they would take the small sentence, not rat out their supplier, and know they were forgiven for the confiscated drugs and would be staked to a new inventory when they got out.

The question was who was "protecting" Carmen—her pimp or her drug dealer or the bar. Was the bar conducting a house of ill fame in addition to serving petrified hot dogs and $1.50 drafts of beer?

CHAPTER FOUR

Preliminary Hearing

Of course, I made the obligatory three calls to Carmen at Roselita's to make sure she would show up for the Preliminary Hearing and to dress like a sixteen year old girl going to church and not a jail bait prostitute on coke. Court was called for 9:00 am but you never knew when the judge would show or when your case would be called. It could be 9:15 or 12:30. Who knew? In any case, I checked in with the court crier but was already No. 6 on the list. Carmen showed at 9:30. The lawyers could sit in the courtroom but their clients had to wait outside, so I went out to sit with Carmen.

"Let's walk a bit." I had to get away from anyone listening. "Look, Carmen. I just got $2000 from someone to represent you. Do you know who that could be?"

"No. But some other lawyer called and said he was going to represent me. I didn't like his tone and Roselita said I should trust you and not someone I didn't know."

"Do you remember who the lawyer was?" "Some kid with an Italian name."

"Did you get his number?"

"Oh yeah. Its in my bag." She produced a handwritten slip.

"Ok. So I'm in as your lawyer. That means you have to trust me. And I need some more information. First, I'm guessing that you work at Tito's and they give you the key to the room upstairs—which is where I suspect you were arrested. I'm also guessing they found coke in bags in the room. I'm also guessing there was a john in the room when you were arrested. Now, I need to know…can you ID the john, what was the name of the cop who arrested you, and where were you taken immediately after you were arrested. If you tell me this, I might be able to get you off completely, but I gotta know these things."

At first, she looked down and gave me the no-look answer mode I'd gotten the first time, but this time with no answer. I could hear the wheels turning though.

"I can't help you if you don't help me. Are you afraid of someone? I can do this without letting anyone know how I know, but I need your help."

Carmen was used to working men, and she was still sizing me up. "Look, Carmen, with this much coke involved they may try you as an adult and you could get some serious time. I can't let that happen." Just about that time, our case was called.

We went into the courtroom where an obese woman with dyed black hair cut into bangs and a short pageboy with bright red lipstick and heavy blue eye shadow told me. "Your case isn't ready? What do you want, next Tuesday or Thursday?" No discussion, no preamble, not even a judge, just the court crier making a ruling. This was Judge Bastoncino's court. He was a lower level juvenile court judge and had argued to a postponement of the case without me.

"Why isn't it ready. Who was the officer?"

"Sorry. I just heard from the District. They need someone from the Attorney General, and the hospital report."

"Ok. Thursday is good for me." But wow! Now there was someone from the Attorney General involved, and a hospital report. Did she mean lab report or did she really mean hospital report? This was getting complicated.

Carmen and I went back to the hallway. "Carmen, with the Attorney General involved this is some kind of bigger case. You've got to tell me what's going on."

"Well. Let me see. I was arrested on the second f loor and me and Louie had done a few lines which were on the nightstand with the other bags. Louie is an older guy, about your age, he's short and thin and has dyed black hair. I think he's a lawyer. He's a regular—every couple weeks and he comes in with a friend who does the other girl— Maria. She's older than me but not much."

"How did they get into the room. They had a key and just opened the door?"

"How did you get into the room?"

"I just get the key from the bartender. I pay him $35."

By now, we were outside. "Can I give you a lift?" She was starting to give me good information and I didn't want it to stop.

"Yeah. Sure."

"How about breakfast?"

"Yeah sure." Besides I wanted to see if this little urchin could wolf down that much breakfast again. It was worth the price of admission.

"Ok. So now you rent the room. Do you split any of what the john gives you with the bartender?"

"No, that's mine. But if I sell some of the coke, I pay him back for the bundle."

"What do you pay a bundle?"

"$250 for 10 bags."

"Who do you sell the coke to?"

"The johns buy one from me at $70, and we have a party."

"Now, when the police came in, where was the john?"

"He was lying on his back next to me."

"Was he done or just getting started?"

"Done."

"Where was his condom?"

"Still on."

"Was the john arrested?"

"I don't know. They took him out of the room and they told me to get dressed and they took me out to the paddy wagon."

"Was the other girl arrested?"

"I don't know."

"The other john?"

"I don't know."

"Did the other john know your john?"

"They come in together."

"What did he look like?"

"Big beefy guy. Curly hair. Handsome, well dressed. Not as old, about 35."

"Where did they take you?"

"To the hospital?"

"What did they do there?"

"Well, one cop stayed with me. They took me to a room, put me on a table and looked up my coochy."

"Did they say anything?"

"No. They just mumbled and wrote stuff down." "Then they took me to juvy in another paddy wagon." "Have you ever been arrested before?"

"Yeah. Under a different name. For making a disturbance. They fined us $25 each and let us go."

"Did they take the condom off your john?"

"I don't know. As I was getting dressed, they were bagging stuff, like the coke, the sheets. Yeah they may have bagged the condom."

We had reached the diner by now, and slid into the back booth again. She was no less quick gobbling the lumberjack special than before—eggs, sausage and bacon, waffles, and a gigantic coke. Like some miniature bird she was consuming at least half her body weight. I could only look longingly at Carmen's breakfast—salt, sugar, cholesterol, enough calories for a week. I had to be content with two soft-boiled eggs and green tea with Splenda.

But she told me some valuable things. At the hospital, they seemed to have been doing a "rape kit." I think they were trying to prove penetration, or collect some DNA. If this was just a prostitution case, this was way beyond the usual procedure. Prostitution is treated as a minor matter with a small fine, but the girl usually gets fingerprinted and a criminal record. This brand ruins her future life prospects if she has any. But a "rape kit" means there was a "sex crime" contemplated.

The only sex crime would be Statutory Rape—an adult having sex with an underage person. There was no question that Carmen looked like jailbait, so someone was building a "sex crime" case. The cops obviously thought so, because they took her straight to " juvy"—the holding cell for juvenile prisoners. They must like the john for stat rape, corrupting and drugs.

Lots of other good stuff. Carmen legally had rented room—that gave her an expectation of privacy. That means that cops had to get a search warrant as well as an arrest warrant before barging in. Otherwise, she walked. With a warrant there would be lots of valuable information. Without, as I said, she walked. I wondered what the probable cause for the raid was. Plus, there were lots of people to testify against for immunity—the johns, the bartender, the owner. And the surveillance camera would back up Carmen's story.

As she finished her breakfast, Carmen chose a cherry and a lemon danish and a milkshake. Did the kid eat between our confabs, or was I her sole source of nutrition?

The presence of the Attorney General's office told me a lot. The drug arrest business was a very competitive one. At one time, there were only local cops working undercover, then the DEA, a federal agency with lots of money, shouldered its way in. The federal drugs laws were much stricter, the federal prosecutors much better paid and could work individual cases more carefully. So they got the bigger and better collars. Then, in 1980, Pennsylvania decided we didn't have enough politicians, so they created the elected office of Attorney General which the winning party would be able to staff with hordes of the party faithful—prosecutors, paralegals, clerks, investigators and unspecified hang around assistants to help with elections. Pennsylvania already had the largest number of elected officials in its legislature—50 senators and 203 representatives, most of whom came from comfortably gerrymandered districts so they not only didn't have to expend much effort or money running for office but didn't have to do anything to justify their existence. Each representative or senator had a full complement of secretaries, aides, assistants as well as home offices, cars, etc. What was the AG doing in Philadelphia tripping over the feet of the local cops and the DEA, and why a vice arrest?

The Attorney General's office was now like teats on a bull. It was able to staff lots of the party faithful as well—incompetent ex local cops, incompetent ex local prosecutors, plenty of unemployed in-laws, and dozens of office staff and paralegals. Supposedly, one of the reasons for its existence was to provide criminal justice for counties or towns too small to have such expertise on their own. Of course, the smaller towns did not share the cost of the office; they only contributed a small percentage and let the tax payers of Philadelphia and Pittsburgh carry the bill. The state of Pennsylvania was carefully gerrymandered to let the small counties control the legislators from Philadelphia and Pittsburgh. As if that were not bad enough, the investigators from the Attorney General's office horned into the territory of Philadelphia County so they could trio over federal and local investigations. Lately, 38 members of the office were named as having exchanged porn among themselves and their friends using state computers. One previous Attorney General went to jail for getting kickbacks in the illegal poker machine game.

So the AG went after little Carmen. Were they on some kind of drug bust, they wouldn't do prostitution? Why were they mucking around in Hispanic North Philly? Or was this political? What were they after? One of the lawyer johns? There were some wires connected somewhere.

CHAPTER FIVE

Preliminary Hearing

On the date of the second hearing, Carmen again showed up— well, almost on time. Without her wedges and makeup and some schoolgirl clothes, she looked petit and vulnerable. We sat patiently until our case was called early— it was a short list that day.

Again, the obese court crier barked out our case name. There was only a uniformed Philadelphia policeman in the witness box. Since I had been told this matter was one for the Attorney General's office, I was surprised.

At the bar of court, I asked the judge (lawyers in court never address each other but direct their questions to the judge) "I understand that this was an AG matter, may I ask what happened to the AG witness?" The judge turned to the assistant DA with raised eyebrows. The ADA, speaking to the judge, said, "We have decided only the one witness was needed to make out the case."

"Alright. Mr. Magen, you have your answer. Let's proceed." I again addressed the court. "Your honor, may I see the 49?" Again the raised eyebrows. Again the ADA. "It's not available yet."

The whole scene so far was beginning to bother me. Juvy court as it is called is the lowest and least competent court in the system. The least competent ADAs are dumped there and the least competent judges are assigned there.

Both positions either reflect the sound judgment of their peers, or were a punishment of some sort. The ADA was a very young somewhat scattered female who seemed inexperienced and nervous. My gray hair and spiffy business suit spoke of way too much experience and she was probably rattled.

Now, the judge was another story. The way to get to be a judge in Philadelphia county essentially costs about $450,000. A lawyer wishing to be a judge usually hired an expert in the process. But this time, the two best "experts" were former elected officials who had gone to jail for felonious acts of bribery committed while in office. These experts spread the money around after taking a hefty fee. Sometimes they paid union bosses, black ward leaders, white ward leaders, ethnic ward leaders, veteran's organizations, you name it. Whatever combination might secure the number of votes to secure the democratic nomination in the primary was carefully calculated to meet the magic number of votes.

Lawyers like to say that those who get A's in law school go back to teach law, those that get B's work for the big firms representing rich clients, those that get C's do the lower level cases, and those that get D's become judges. It was no exception in Philadelphia. Today's judge was a husky, slow-witted, go with the f low guy—Judge O'Connell. He got his judgeship and he never had to work again. In Juvy, he was done his list at 12:30 and would be on the golf course at 1:30. Today, he had a list of 10 preliminary hearings and we were the third called. It was 10:15.

Now, preliminary hearings are not a formal trial. The law requires that the ADA prove that there is sufficient evidence to avoid a dismissal. It is called a prima facie case. Just bare bones to have the matter set down for a regular trial. The strategy of the ADA is to reveal as little of the case as possible so the defense lawyer cannot use a few extraneous facts to pick the case apart. The defense lawyer, at this stage, knows almost nothing and wants to learn as much as he can about the facts. Issues which do not have a direct bearing on the prima facie case are usually excluded from the defense lawyer's inquiry.

So the ADA began: "What is your name?"

"Officer Thomas O'Leary, 12th district, badge number 2246."

"What did you observe on May 17, 2015 at or about 7:35pm?"

He read from a paper of what looked like handwritten notes. "I entered the taproom known as 'Tito's' at 1747 North Fifth Street, and went to the second f loor. I observed the defendant in bed with a male who was lying on top of her. As I entered, the defendant screamed. The male jumped up. We arrested the female for prostitution. In the course of the arrest, I observed what I believed to be the remains of several lines of cocaine on the nightstand. As a result, I searched the immediate area and found what appeared to be eight bags of cocaine in the defendant's purse along with $170 in cash. I instructed her to get dressed. When she had done so, I took her down to St. Christopher's Hospital in my custody."

"Your witness, Mr. Magen."

The ADA had not made out a case for prostitution, and I should have simply moved to dismiss. However, the better ADA would simply have her re-arrested and Carmen would be back on trial three weeks later. I wanted to find out what I could and use my leverage on the judge to let me ask what I wanted. I was sure the judge knew a case had not been made out, but who knew what this neanderthal would do. "Officer O'Leary. Good morning." We always said good morning.

I don't know why. Maybe to put him at ease. "Good morning, sir." He was not at ease. "Was the man arrested also?"

"I don't know. I just took the defendant to the hospital." "How did you know the cocaine was hers?"

"I saw that it was within her reach and in her purse." "How did you know it was her purse?"

"I saw her ID in her wallet."

"How could you see inside her purse?" "I opened it."

"So then you knew she was a minor—sixteen years old." "Yes. That's why I took her to the hospital for a rape kit." "You didn't think she'd been raped, did you?"

"No. She showed no signs of struggle. We needed to prove penetration for a charge of Statutory Rape."

"So. You wanted to prove Statutory Rape against the man?" "Objection!" The ADA objected because this had nothing to do

with the prostitution charge against the defendant, but did bear on the case against the john.

"Sustained. Not relevant."

"Thank you, your honor. How did you know to go to this room to arrest the defendant?"

"I had been solicited by her previously." Uh-oh. I just made a mistake. The latest arrest didn't prove prostitution, but the solicitation might. Well, I had to blunder ahead. It was going to come out anyway, but the DA's office might not know to charge the early solicitation as well as this one. If they did, then they had a case.

"Oh, so you had seen the defendant before."

"Yes. On information received, I went to the taproom on April 29, 2014 at 7:30pm and saw her sitting at the bar. After some conversation, she asked me if I liked young girls. I said I did. She said she could be available. I asked what it would cost. She said $150, but no BJ, and no anal. I told her I'd have to get the money and return. She said she'd be looking for me."

Uh-oh. He had made out the case for prostitution. Very pat. Well-rehearsed. This was a vice cop, not a narc. It was also fishy. I didn't believe him and would look at the tapes. Alright, let's see what else I could get. "Was there an Attorney General's officer with you?"

"Objection!" The ADA did not want to get another witness who might contradict the first one. I appealed to the judge, after all they would have to let me eventually.

"Your honor, this case was postponed because they needed an AG officer. I would like to at least find out if he was there and if this officer saw him participating in the arrest. Besides, the presence of another witness is absolutely relevant."

"Objection sustained. Not relevant." The judge had it wrong, but there was little I could do.

"Who was the man with the defendant?"

"I don't know." He blurted this out over the ADA's objection. "You never got his name and he was guilty of statutory rape." "No."

"Alright. How did you go into the taproom?"

"I went to the bartender and asked where Flora was. Flora was the name she had given me. He told me she was on the second floor. That she had taken the room."

"She had taken the room? What did that mean?"

"She was required to give him $35 for the room, and then got the key. That's what she had said."

Aha. The gods were smiling. He had just told me that she had "rented" the room and therefore had an expectation of privacy. It was her room. If the cops wanted in the room, they would need a warrant. I could file a motion and get at least the arrest thrown out. The prior solicitation might be a problem, but this arrest was out.

"Did you have a warrant to enter the room."

"No." I could hear the other defense lawyers awaiting their turn to try their case shifting in their seats. I had made a good point.

"Did you take the condom from the room?"

"I don't know. I didn't know there was a condom." I got away with that question. The ADA was looking at the notes for the next case and was not paying attention.

"Who took the suspected cocaine?" "I don't know. I didn't."

"How do you know it was cocaine?" A lab test for the cocaine usually took a few weeks and was not available for most preliminary hearings.

"We did a field test." That was good enough for the proof of cocaine at this level. They'd have the lab test for trial.

"You say 'we.' Who was 'we'?" Aha. Now I could get at least another name. "That was Thomas Martin of the AG's office." The ADA was snippy. "Happy now?"

"Yes. Thank you for small favors."

The judge did not like the bickering and chided both of us. "That's enough, counselors. Anything else, Mr. Magen?"

"Let me check my notes…Oh yes, one more thing. I see that you have been referring to a piece of paper, officer. Can I see it?" It's absolutely proper to request to see any notes the witness refers to while testifying.

"Objection!" From the ADA.

"Your honor, it is absolutely proper for me to see any document the witness refers to to refresh his recollection."

The ADA was defending the request. "Your honor, this is an incomplete 49 and is still confidential at this point."

The judge was wavering and didn't want to disappoint the ADA; me he could care less about. So the judge addressed the officer. "Are these your own notes?"

"Well. In part, yes."

"Did you refer to these notes to aid in your testimony?" "Yes, but they are incomplete and not all my notes."

I addressed the judge who was now restless and didn't want to make a mistake. "Yes, counselor, go ahead."

"Are those notes typewritten on a 49 form?" Obviously we all could see that.

"Some of these are your notes, some are those of other officers, is that right?"

"Yes. Some are mine."

"Did you read yours before and during the time you were testifying? Obviously, we allow that."

"Then, may I see them?" Now the judge had to make a ruling. "Counselor, I'm going to have to rule against you. They are mixed

with other notes." Absolutely the wrong ruling! He had no idea what he was doing. This is basic law school stuff.

"Then, your honor, I ask that these notes be marked exhibit D-1 and held under seal, pending my appeal of this issue." I was not a friend of the judge now. I was calling his expertise into question and exposing his stupidity to the other judges. People didn't do this in juvy court. So what the hell! I was too old to get into trouble.

"Alright counsel." I could hear him grinding his teeth from about fifteen feet. "Anything else?"

"No. That will be all."

The judge bound the defendant over for court on all counts and gave us a calendar date six weeks away.

CHAPTER SIX

Post Preliminary Hearing— Hello Louis

As we walked out of the courtroom, I asked Carmen to stay for a few minutes while I jotted down some thoughts on what I had learned. First, there was the involvement of the AG's office—were they in this arrest or not? Since I wasn't allowed to see the 49, I couldn't be sure even if they were there or not. And the elusive 49? First, it was delayed and next, I wasn't allowed to see it. Either the judge had erred on the law or he was party to concealing it from me.

Second: the case seems to have been started with a prior solicitation by Carmen on the vice cop who had testified. The second confrontation with the cop was definitely lacking a search warrant, but the first seemed like a good bust at the time. Would the DA make a mistake and only charge the second one, or would they wise up and correct? Since the first confrontation had not actually been charged in this second arrest, would the DA know how to connect everything? In my humble opinion, I think they would have to rearrest and give her a new preliminary hearing, but that was a debatable issue. In any case, without a warrant, this second arrest charging coke found at the scene could be suppressed. The room had been "rented" to Carmen, she was entitled to an expectation of privacy and the finding of cocaine would drop out of the case. So far, so good.

And what of the john? Who was he and why could I learn his name? The issue that he might be an owner, in whole or in part, of the coke was an issue. If he paid for it, he would be charged with possession. Was he being kept out of the case? Did he appear in the 49 and then was removed? Why not arrest him too and keep his case to be tried with her case? Especially if he could be charged with statutory rape. All good questions. I'd have to do some more research and investigation. I got up to go and found Carmen listening idly to some music on her earphones. It took a few waves to get her attention to leave. We started to walk down the hall, when I saw Judge Bastoncino walking with his law clerk in the opposite direction. Out of the blue, Carmen waved to the judge and said with a smug smile, "Oh hi, Louie." I thought the judge was going to fall over. He literally staggered, looking at Carmen, then at me and finally was able to blurt out "Hello, Flora," and passed on.

Ayi Chihuahua! I almost staggered myself. Could it be? Yes, it must. Judge Bastoncino was Carmen's Louie, the would-be, or should I say, should have been co-defendant in Carmen's arrest. He was the missing john. And since he was still walking the halls of Juvy, he hadn't been arrested and somehow he had not been mentioned in the latest 49 or acknowledged by the arresting cop. And the judge had prevented me from learning who he was at the Preliminary Hearing.

Very interesting. This case was now going to be fun.

Judge Bastoncino was a poster child for the evil effects of judges not selected on a merit system. For years he had been an embarrassment to the legal profession. As a lawyer, he had been tossed a few minor cases by his more successful buddies. Eventually, somehow, he had been nominated for a judgeship and won. As the judge in charge of assignments to the various court rooms, it was apparent those in charge had discovered rather quickly his incompetence, he sunk lower and lower on the scale of assignments. He had been in Juvy for many years now and even there he was a calendar judge—one whose sole responsibility was to assign cases out to other judges to try.

However, his meager career accomplishments did not prevent him from acquiring a case of "black robe disease." That affliction was carried by mediocre judges who enjoyed lording it over lawyers who came before him. Not only did he demand great humility from ordinary lawyers and their clients, but he insisted on belittling everyone publicly. On occasion, he would mete out small fines for minor indiscretions or breach of etiquette.

A certain group of lawyers, however, were able to court judges of this sort, who never picked up the tab for the drinks or meals, and were frequent guests at local golf clubs and office parties.

It was rumored that, while in practice as a young lawyer, he shared space in an office suite with a small group of lawyers who made him the butt of their many jokes. The sleazier part of the rumor was that he was active in procuring call girls or strippers for the co-tenants of the suite and their clients, and friends.

Although I was only a very occasional practitioner in Juvy, I knew to be on my guard around him. And now, Carmen had given me this golden nugget of information—he was her john and he committed statutory rape and snorted coke with her. What's more, he was a Juvy judge—his job was to handle cases involving these very similar offenses. While I was reveling in these delicious thoughts, it struck me. I had no evidence. No one would believe Carmen, and it might be even harder for her if she made that accusation. I, too, was in trouble, the esteemed judge might be able to guess that I now knew his secret. Of course, it might give me power, but it also made me a marked man. Who knew what his supporters, those who helped him onto the bench, might do? Still, I liked my odds. But I needed to develop more information from Carmen and elsewhere.

As we worked, I cautioned Carmen. "Don't talk until we are out of the building." She stared straight ahead and walked. Once in the car, I said, "So Louie was your john when you were arrested?"

"Yes, and before that, too."

"Wow! Do you know who Louie is?" "Some lawyer he said."

"Well, he is Tomaso Bastoncino, Judge in the Juvenile Court System."

"Whoa, he's a judge? No way."

"Yes, way. Now this really complicates things, but it is your get out of jail free card if we play this right. Do you understand?"

"Yeah. I rat him out, I walk."

"Good. Only trouble is no one is gonna believe you. You're a little sparrow and he's a big bird and well connected. So I can't go after him unless I've got some more proof. And that begins with you."

"Is there something else in this for me? Or if I just plead can I bring this thing to an end?"

"Okay. Good question. It depends. Let's see what happens."

"If I tell you, you have to promise not to do anything without telling me. I don't want no more trouble, and I don't want you to sell me down the river for a little bump for yourself."

"Fair enough. First, I am your lawyer. Anything you tell me I can't reveal to anyone else. Confidential lawyer-client privilege."

"I got that, but I can still get screwed in other ways. And probation isn't so bad—I get no adult criminal record, and I walk with a little probation, and a juvy conviction doesn't go on my crimmy." She knew the lingo now and was talking like the toughest guy on the street. "That's no sweat."

"But if I bring down the judge and the big boys investigate—the FBI, or Internal Affairs, not only do you walk but you get to sue everyone for a coverup—denial of your civil rights."

"I can't afford all that."

"If I win you some money in a civil rights case, I get counsel fees from the other side. But I have to win."

"Wow! The feds, the big boys—interested in little me." "Big time with a perv judge in Juvenile Court."

"Big time!"

"Okay—you tell me everything. Deal?" "Deal. Ok, now you tell me."

"Louie had seen me a few times. $150 a piece. Those kind of johns like me."

"What do you mean those kind of johns?"

"Little guys. They like little girls. Makes them feel big and they get to boss us around." Tomaso Bastoncino was small and slight, about 5'5" and about 130 pounds.

"Did the other girl that got arrested, did she know him?" "Some. We sat at the bar together. She was a big girl with big tits,

a big ass, and dumb as a rock. The big guys liked her. I don't know her real name, but they called her Sheila. She looked Irish—big rosy cheeks, blonde hair and white skin."

"Do you know where she lives?"

"Kinda. In Fishtown, near the new casino." "Do you know the john she was with?"

"All I know is Frankie, he's a lawyer, too. Big husky fella, curly dark hair. Very funny. Likes to laugh."

"Did they usually come together?"

"Usually. Frankie has a big car and usually drives there. The bartender seems to kiss his ass when he comes in. Not so much with Louie."

"So far so good. Do you know what kind of car?" "A big Lincoln with those fancy hubcaps."

"Can you draw them for me?"

"I'll try when we get to my place."

"Now. The coke. Where did that come from?"

"Some Spanish guy delivers it every couple days and gives it to the bartender. He locks it in the safe and gives me a bundle when I pay him for the last bundle. $250 a bundle."

"So you pay $250, and sell 10 bags for $70 a piece."

"No. The johns pay me $70 a piece. On the steet, it goes for $50 to $100 a piece, but the johns want to make me happy." "Those cameras around the bar. Do they work?"

"You bet they do. The bartender's boss goes into the closet and watches them every few weeks."

"Is he the owner?"

"No. Just another Spanish guy."

"The bartender or the boss, are they puertoricano?"

"No. Probably Dominican."

"Good so far. Now, did, uh…Louie ejaculate?"

"Uh, what…Oh, you mean pop his cork? Yeah, he's like a teenager. After I f luff him up a bit, he's quick." "Yeah, but inside you?"

"No. We use rubbers."

"What happened to the rubber? Can we get some DNA?"

"I think it fell on the f loor during the arrest. He had finished but was still on top of me breathing heavy when they came in."

"Did they take the rubber with them when they took you?" "I think so. I don't remember."

"Okay, so no DNA."

"Yeah, but…" she giggled, "when I say but, I mean butt. My finger had been up his butt. That's what he liked. He may have been a bit ACDC."

"So what happened to your finger?"

"I wiped it on my thong when I picked it up from the f loor. He had ripped it so I just put it in my purse. I was going to stitch it up at home. But I haven't gotten to it."

"You haven't washed it yet?" "No. Not yet."

"Wonderful! So you went commando down to St. Chris, and back to juvy?"

"Yup, and it was a cold night. My coochy like to froze." "What else about Louie?"

"Yeah, he had a mole removed on his back. He had a bandaid on it and he told me not to touch it."

"Great. Now, did the cops know you were under 18?"

"Of course, they looked in my purse where the bags of coke were." "Did they take your purse or just the coke?"

"No, just the coke and the money." "What money?"

"$220, and they kept that, too."

"Now the bags, who opened the bags of coke?"

"I did that."

"So any fingerprints?"

"The nightstand where the lines of coke were, he may have touched that."

"Carmen, you've been great. Do you mind if we go to the hospital to get your records before breakfast?"

"Oh, I love these breakfasts. Can we do it after?"

"Okay. I don't know where you put all these breakfasts."

"I already know what I want. I never can get this by myself." "Okay, what?"

"I want eggs over and pork roll with cream chipped beef and two blueberry muffins with a strawberry milkshake."

"Is that all?"

During breakfast, since it was late in the morning, we were alone at the rear of the diner. I had to ask. "How did you get into this life? Were you abused?"

"My mom always had some guy over and they were doing it in her room. I usually slept in her room, but when the guys were over, I slept on the couch. I could hear them."

"Did they ever take a shot at you?"

"Yeah, they did, and the guys in school did. I kind of learned what they needed. Usually a hand job or a blow job and they left me alone. When they didn't, I just like turned off my mind and hoped they were over quick. It wasn't long before I got some money for it.

"I learned when they really wanted it, which they usually did, I felt they were idiots. If I gave it to them, I could do whatever I wanted. Laugh at them, make them buy me things, whatever. I could even make them pop their corks whenever I wanted. They were easy.

"And I got what I wanted. I got some serious coin stashed." "I hope you've put it in the bank or something."

"Of course, I worked to get it and I'm gonna keep it."

I looked with envy as she gobbled her breakfast, while I had from a bowl of bran cereal and some green tea.

We got in the car and drove to St. Christopher's Hospital medical records. We walked up to the counter and waited until the lady came up. "Hello, we're here for Carmen Jacinto's records. She was here April 17."

"Alright, show me your ID and sign the HIPAA release." As we handed in her ID and the signed form, the lady went into the file room for quite a while.

"Sorry, no such record."

I turned to Carmen. "Are you sure this was the hospital?" "Yeah sure. Sixth and Erie."

I turned to the lady. "She was here for a pelvic exam incident to a rape charge. I'm sure she was here. Would you have the record for that kind of visit?"

"If it happened in this hospital, it would be here." "Even if it was a police matter?"

"Any contact with this hospital is in these files."

Then, I knew we were in for some trouble. The revised police 49 was one thing, hospital records were something else.

CHAPTER SEVEN

Discovery, Motion and Fears

That evening, I sat at my desk with many thoughts rushing through my head. I had to sort them out. In the criminal process, it was customary to prepare what is called a discovery motion to file as early as possible meant to get the presecutor to disclose a number of pieces of evidence he may have which either tend to prove a defendant not guilty or maybe used to cross-examine prosecution witnesses. Some facts do not fall in either category and the prosecutor may refuse to disclose them. It is a fundamentally unfair piece of criminal procedure that prevents the defendant from preparing for trial. In a civil case, the parties can compel each other to disclose anything remotely relevant to the case or even take the deposition of any person who is minimally connected to the case. In a criminal case, the defendant is left with very little to go on. One mechanism is the discovery motion. Often, the judge will bend over backwards to be fair to the defense and require the prosecution to turn over far more than he might be required to. Often, the prosecutor recognizes this tremendous power and simply turns his file over to the defense. I sensed there was some kind of coverup afoot. I was not going to roll over and plead out my client without a fight.

In the discovery motion, I usually threw in the kitchen sink and asked for everything I could think of. Here, though, I somehow felt that I did not want to show what I was thinking. So I drew the motion to ask for things any decent lawyer would ask for: the names of the two johns, the condom, the rape kit, the tapes from the bar, any exterior tapes showing the johns' car, the name of the bartender, the ownership documents for the bar, fingerprints, DNA, all police at the scene of the arrest, the cocaine packets, all police reports by the Phila cops or the AG's office and all drafts of those reports.

There were two problems with all of this. First, by asking for this information, I was revealing what my strategy might be and also showing what I knew so far. These might be things the DA had not thought of. The second problem, and far worse, was that this evidence was perishable. That is, it might not be around for very long and could easily get lost or manage to disappear. This is especially bad if the arresting police officer had already tried to conceal most of it in his report. If I was looking at a coverup, I had to know who was involved. I knew I could expect the District Attorney's office to show my discovery requests and, while the Police Report would not bury evidence, some of individual police might.

I also wanted to send a message to anyone on the outside that I was snooping around and might look too closely into some of their affairs. I also wanted to mask my inquiries by asking for a few things that did not exist or were totally irrelevant—a bit of misinformation.

To that end, I looked up the Liquor Control Board ("LCB") records to see who the owner and designated manager of the bar was. These facts were contained in regularly kept LCB files and kept up to date every two years. This yielded some interesting information. The "owner" was a corporation owned by a woman—"Margaret Mary O'Leary" and her business address was a lawyer's office. The manager was Emilio Puente. There was no financing information indicating the bar claimed to have bought for $100,000 in cash, three years ago. The real estate records showed $100,000 was the purchase price for the real estate alone. This was interesting because the liquor license was worth about $25,000 alone. However, this discrepancy could also have been a clerical error.

However, if you don't ask, you never learn. So I added the names of Ms. O'Leary, the corporation, and Mr. Puente to the discovery request. I also added a few random hispanic and irish sounding names just in case.

These days, the DA's office was able to confiscate any property involved in a crime—especially drug trafficking—so this put the ownership of the bar at risk if the owner had knowledge of the illegal activity on the premises.

I rushed to get the entire discovery motion typed up and filed. The court would schedule a session with the DA's office to see what the DA either had and would produce, didn't have, or had and refused to produce. That would occur in a week. I knew I was causing a lot of trouble for one little hooker on coke, but if you don't ask, they don't tell.

35

CHAPTER EIGHT

Internal Affairs

Over the years, in my practice, I had a number of dealings with the Internal Affairs Division ("IAD")—the very much feared department of the police that investigated the police themselves. I had, for a time, represented the Police Union and defended a few errant cops, and I had reported a number of bad cops in my job as criminal defense attorney. The investigators from IAD were hated and feared by the rest of the cops. In the course of my dealings I had made a good friend of Lieutenant Mehle who was known as such a straight arrow by the cops that his nickname was "Twang."

Since I suspected a coverup of the Judge's and the cop's involvement in the bar's activities, and the AG's interest in my poor little Carmen, I knew a little sniff by Twang would put the fear of God into anyone not in a state of grace.

So I called Twang, although I would never call him that, to try to involve him in the process and spring a bit more information.

His given name was Horatio, which unfortunately suggested that he be called either "Whore" or "Rat" by his enemies. So I called him "Lt. Mehle."

After exchanging a few pleasantries and a few reminiscences of our previous matters together, I told him the story of my Carmen. I explained that I thought a Phila Police Department or an AG office coverup was involved. After some thought, the good Lt. Mehle began to analyze the facts.

"So your client is charged with prostitution and coke, but you think the cops are burying the evidence from her john and the other girl and her john, because one's a judge and the other's a big deal lawyer. You think the evidence as to them will disappear.

"On the other hand, your girl is a criminal defendant without evidence or much credibility due to her choice of medication and profession."

Twang had a keen mind and could cut to the chase. I just wanted a discrete inquiry from him to shake up the troops and I promised him enough information to give him a well-publicized collar.

Since Mama Mehle didn't raise no dummies, Twang agreed as a minimum to contact the AG and the Police District Captain about some interviews for the cops involved. Cops burying arrests of muckity- mucks was always a good case for him, but he was not going further until he had much better evidence. I emailed him a brief summary of what I had told him with names, dates and places, but of course left anything out which would breach attorney-client privilege.

CHAPTER NINE

Mr. Lynch

About mid-morning, I got a telephone call from Liam Lynch, Esq., could we meet? Mr. Lynch was an old time liquor lawyer. Everyone knew him and generally liked him. His specialty if not his only practice involved representing people buying and selling bars, taverns, and any establishment serving alcoholic beverages. He had very good relations with the LCB bureaucracy and could resolve problems of licensing, violations and other matters quickly and quietly. Although the bar business was often rife with involvement in other unsavory matters, including bookmaking, illegal poker machines, money laundering, etc., Liam himself had a good reputation and was trusted and respected by the rest of the legal community although he was also the father confessor to a number of bad guys.

We met for lunch at one of his clubs in a private booth. The good thing about being in Mr. Lynch's business was that he never had to pick up a tab and was owed favors every place he ate or drank. The food at his club was known to be particularly good. It would be a good time to stretch my diet.

"So, Liam, what's going on at the Elephant Room?" This was a private men's club for high net worth individuals that rented space in a hotel I represented. The young men of the club had decided to call in some strippers on occasion—an illegal act that passed scrutiny. The girls were soliciting tips—an illegal act which passed scrutiny. The girls were providing sexual acts of varying degrees of depravity—illegal acts which also passed scrutiny. Eventually, however, one of the drunken gentlemen of high net worth assaulted one of the ecdysiasts who then complained loudly and counter-assaulted the young gentleman—all of which caused the hotel guests, and as a result the hotel security to intervene just ahead of the police.

The matter was resolved because Liam and I were able to cooperate by compensating the girl, sternly rebuking the club membership, increasing the club's rent and richly rewarding the hotel security guard for his discretion. Everyone went home mildly unhappy except for the hotel security guard, which is always a sign of a good settlement.

Midway through a lunch of excellent crab imperial and cherrystones, a side of creamed spinach for all of which the club was celebrated and a shared bottle of crisp Pino Grigio, Liam started backing into the reason for our meeting. "You know, Ms. O'Leary is a secretary in my office by now." By now, I did. "She is actually my son's secretary now although she came to us directly from Little Flower." A Catholic girls high school which over the years has produced countless competent, hard working, loyal, legal secretaries. There must be a special place in heaven for such secretaries. No NFL team covets a Penn State linebacker more than a Philadelphia lawyer covets a Little Flower legal secretary. "Can we speak totally off the record and I think it will be worth your while?"

"Of course, Liam. I'm listening."

Of course I was listening. At this point, I had what is known in the legal profession as "bubkis"—or nothing. Somehow, I had shaken the tree and a few peaches had fallen.

Mr. Lynch was dressed like an english country squire. Even though today was getting warmer, he wore a heavy tan and green plaid tweed three piece suit. The vest actually had lapels on it and a gold watch chain hung across his ample midsection. His shirt was a custom made english shirt with a starched white collar and a yellow and green striped body with french cuffs. His tie was what they call a club tie, meaning it had symbols of some school or club stitched in embroidery onto an amber field.

I kind of knew where he was going with this but I knew just listening was the best course.

After a few fidgets and false starts, he managed to begin. "Ms. O'Leary has been with us for many years. I had her work for my son, Peter. I was hoping she might keep him under control and make a lawyer out of him. He is impulsive and wants to move too far too fast. But he was a bit too much to handle.

"He started to attract some of the wrong clients and wanted to please them at very high fees. As we know, if you lie down with dogs, you get up with f leas. As you also know, the LCB has strict rules against people with criminal records getting liquor licenses or managing liquor establishments.

"He got in worse than I could imagine. He let Margaret Mary become the title owner of bars for a few bad people. They bought these bars for cash and disclosed a price of about one half to the LCB. Then he had a few puppets named as designated managers. As you can hear already, he had broken about half a dozen LCB rules. But for this he got a healthy fee upfront and regular cash payments from the real owners to launder their drug money.

"Neither he nor Margaret Mary knew this was a brothel or a drug dispensary; but if this were to get out it would kill our practice, my son's future, and subject him to large fines, if not disbarment. I need to keep a lid on this."

"Liam, I think it's worse than you thought. First, I believe your son may be a husky young man with curly hair who drives a big gray Lincoln with custom hubcaps. I also suspect he was in the bar on the night of the arrest and was caught by the police with a blonde prostitute en f lagrante delicto, in the saddle as it were."

Poor Liam blanched. I had taken a shot in the dark, and bagged a moose. With a heavy heart for Liam, but not entirely without some relish, I told him that his son seems not yet to have been identified by the police, but that there were ample witnesses and possibly a CD showing him with the judge on the night of the arrest.

"Mr. Magen, I am not entirely without some resources. I have in my possession the CD and it seems Peter had the forethought to avoid the camera."

"What do you want, Liam? I have no wish to harm you or your son."
"Since it may aid your defense, I will give you the original copy of the CD.

But I want you to avoid pressing the discovery of my son or Ms. O'Leary."

"That's fine as far as it goes, Liam. But you must realize that the DA's office may seek forfeiture of the bar, the real estate and the liquor license. With or without my help, they will claim the owner knew of the illegal activity going on. Our testimony will cinch it up, of course. I need something more."

"What do you propose?"

"The bar is lost as soon as the DA's bureaucracy goes after it. Since it will only proceed against the property itself, you could probably avoid adverse publicity and cover your son's involvement by simply surrendering it. Since you don't actually own it, the only loser is the felon who owns it secretly."

"I see your point so far."

"With your resources, you could sell this bar and transfer all the assets before the DA even figures out that it is there. I propose that my client get a percent of the sale. After all, she could sue your secretary, your son and the corporation for luring her into a life of sex trafficking. Then your son would have to reveal the true owner's name. Ya da, ya da."

"What do you want?

"I need more information from your son about the owner etc, and how the place works."

"No. We know nothing about that."

"The only remaining witness to implicate your son would be the prostitute he was with. I don't believe she was charged or if they even took her name. I'll have to let you know what they know."

"We have some work to do. Give me a call when you know something." Liam and I finished our excellent crab imperial, and finished it off with an espresso. I knew I had pushed a bit but I also knew he had no choice. Although not extremely credible, my client could prove very costly to him. It was not worth the risk.

CHAPTER TEN

Mehle – Second Phone Call

It was about 2 in the afternoon when I got a telephone call from Lt. Mehle. "Mr. Magen, glad I could catch you in. I sent out a few feelers concerning your matter as we had discussed and got back something that makes me more than a bit curious."

"I've gotten a few things too, but, please, let me know."

"The most disturbing thing is that the police department can't release the 49 to me yet. They say it is being revised. So I asked the Captain to preserve the officer's original notes. When he asked the Sgt. for them, I was told they would be a bit delayed as well. Those 49's are supposed to be done the next day. It's been two weeks now and it kills their credibility."

"As I told you, I think they're trying to juggle the facts to protect a few people. Maybe the judge, maybe the bar owner."

"It sounds like it. What have you got?"

"The real owner of the bar was a drug dealer. The name on the LCB license is a stand-in."

"That's illegal, but not a surprise. Most of these low rent bars are merely launderers. But I'm not interested in doing the LCB's work. I could be interested in the drug dealer if he's bought a few police. I did find out that this Philadelphia cop is not vice, he's a narc. Why he's making vice arrests sounds hinky. I don't like hinky."

"I can tell you he didn't have probable cause so I'm pretty sure my client's arrest gets tossed. I don't know what they were doing in there. Who was this AG cop in on the arrest?"

"It turns out he is in from Coatsville and he was working on a drug bust out there. He may be the confidential informant for this case. That's why they don't want to reveal his name and why the 49 is being revised so often."

"Could this be one drug gang ratting out another?"

"That could be."

"Thank you, Lt., I'll get back to you if I've got something else."

CHAPTER ELEVEN

Mexican DNA

It was becoming increasingly obvious that I needed to tie the judge to my client's thong. I pondered those choice of words carefully. I needed the judge's DNA in the worst way or, better yet, the best way. The judge was a well-known mooch who played golf with his cronies in the criminal defense business on their memberships. Most of them belonged to a golf club just inside the city. If I could pick up a glass or a cigarette butt properly documented, I could get the bastard.

My first call was to Al Covarubias, a nice young lawyer with an office in center city and in the hispanic neighborhood out on Rising Sun Avenue.

"Al, Dave Magen, here. I wanted to ask you for a reference." "Sure Dave, what can I do?"

"I need a good hispanic detective for some surveillance. I figured you'd know one."

"Sure, no problem. I have a really reliable fellow. Former narc from Mexico, military trained. Cooperated with DEA on a number of busts so they got him a green card and sent him undercover on both sides of the border. He's retired from field work and has his own agency now." "Perfect. Let me have his number." I called Gino Nuncio immediately and set up a meet that afternoon at a coffee shop on Broad Street.

"Mr. Nuncio, you come well recommended."

Gino Nuncio was a short stocky guy with swarthy skin. He definitely had a military bearing in his neat office-casual dress, and salt and pepper crew cut. Maybe, he channeled cop a bit too much for what I needed.

Gino nodded politely and asked what he could do.

"I've got a rather prominent guy who has committed stat rape on my client. I need to get his DNA to tie him into a few pieces of evidence. I need you to impersonate a golf course worker or a country club waiter on a Saturday or Sunday and pick up his cigar or cigarettes and his drink glass. I need pictures proving where you get it and an affidavit detailing your actions. What do you think?"

After a few minutes, nodding his head from side to side as if dramatizing his role in his head, he said, "Probably a piece of cake. In an all white men's club, we Mexicans are almost invisible. I could blend in with the staff in plain daylight. But I'll need to get their uniforms and get access to a golf cart…and I'll need a picture of the subject."

"Before you agree, I have to tell you we are going after Judge Bastoncino, from the Philadelphia Juvenile Court System, my client is Carmen Jacinto and the bar known as Tito's Place may be involved. I don't want any hesitation or conflicts of interest if this matter should blow up and I need your testimony."

"Yeah. I know Tito's. It's a beat up old hang out for dirtbags—no love lost there. I don't know any Carmen Jacinto. And I certainly don't mind bringing down a juvy judge doing little spanish girls. So no. No problemo. And in answer to your next question, can I look like a campesino? I spent 15 years doing that. Just get me a uniform and a golf cart. Now, I charge $500 per day, and $200 for an affidavit. I need $250 up front."

Gino was certainly "squared away" as the military guys put it, so it was a go.

The next day, dressed in white guys' golf clothes, which was not too hard for me, I had closets and drawers full of them for a very simple reason. I chose the khaki Greg Norman shorts and the forest green Golden Bear logo shirt. A St. Louis baseball cap completed the picture and shielded my eyes. I, too, was invisible as I walked in the club. I wandered out to the golf club and began to wander around. I looked over the grounds crew and they mostly wore Dickie's green work pants, worn-out sneakers and green military fatigue shirts—easy enough. The wait staff who were the busboys wore white jackets and pants from a commercial laundry. The waiter and waitresses wore a customized shirt with the golf club logo. They all wore black shoes. Since the white commercial uniforms were neatly stacked in the staff locker room, I purloined (temporarily) a set that was Gino's size.

So far, so good. I then took one of the golf carts from the maintenance shed where it was charging for the next day and hid it behind the maintenance building on the third hole on the course.

I met Gene the next day and gave him the busboy clothes which fit decently and gave him some money to buy the green outfit. We agreed to meet Saturday morning at the golf club parking lot. In the meantime, I handed over a few newspaper photos of the judge, but I intended to point out the judge in the parking lot on Saturday. I explained that I needed photos of the judge on the tee with his friends with a newspaper front page. A few more shots of him smoking, and a few shots of him throwing the butt away and a shot of the cigar butt in situ—where he had thrown it. I also needed a picture of him drinking with his friends and a picture of his glass—in situ—before my invisible busboy picked it up.

Gene nodded knowledgeably all during my instructions. He then took out of his pocket a miniscule camera and said, "No sweat."

On Friday, I called the Pro Shop and asked if the group with Mr. Bastoncino was full. I knew the junior pro was scanning down the computer listings. "Ah, here it is. Yeah, it's a full foursome at 10:32." Just to keep up the pretense, I asked when the next opening was. It wouldn't open until 12:45. Fine, a full day with slow play all foursomes.

I met Gene at 9:30 in the course parking lot and positioned myself to watch the golfers leaving the lot and going to the pro shop. Gene was already in his work clothes and had his golf cart parked under some nearby trees. Finally, Bastoncino came past. I pointed, Gene nodded and left my car.

I probably shouldn't have done it, but I made a tee time for myself with two guys I was used to playing with at my course. I was a little wound up from my detective work and my shots off the practice range were scattered and my putts on the practice green had minds of their own.

At my tee time of 12:15, I was joined by Howard Rosenberg a retired gynecologist, and Ken Weiss, a semi-retired CPA. I was playing terribly. My mind was elsewhere until we reached the third hole. I was looking for my ball in the pine straw where I had put a small slice with my drive when my phone rang. I was still a pretty big hitter, so the ball was 250 yards off the tee and well beyond Howard and Ken. Howard usually had his drive about 170, followed with a 170 yard three wood. But then the game changed. He was deadly from 100 yards out. I answered the call, although I knew this was really impolite and golf is a game all about politeness.

The caller ID was Gene's phone. I answered and he whispered, "Got the butt and the snaps." and he hung up. A weight fell from my shoulders. I punched the ball off the pine straw to about 50 yards off the green, but Howard was already on the green in 3 and so was Ken. I lobbed a sand wedge to about 20 feet out of the hole and lagged up for a gimme 5. Ken also got a 5, but, dammit, Howard sank a 10 footer for a par.

By the turn, my game was still a bit off and I had to spring for the hot dogs and gatorade all around. When we got to the twelfth, I was holding my own when the phone rang again with Gino's ID. With many apologies, I took the call to hear another tense whisper. "Glass acquired, snaps clear." The thirteenth hole was a long par 5. My kind of hole. I blasted a 270 yard drive down the middle, hit a 220 3 wood to the edge of the trap and nursed a wedge to within 3 feet. Since I was putting for a bird, no one could concede the putt. After watching Howard and Ken roll in a few weak 6's, I stood over the putt. "Kerplunk." I never looked back and swept off the back nine, the whole match and the press on 18 for the entire enchilada. The golf gods had smiled.

The late lunch and beer in the club house were particularly delightful because Ken had to pay. As a CPA, he was notoriously tight with a buck and it was rumored that he held a nickel so tight as the buffalo shat. Well, the buffalo's back years ago.

Gino's affidavit and two large kitchen baggies were on my desk in 2 days along with his bill for $700. I sent him a check for $1000 with profuse thanks.

I hand carried the evidence with the stickers still affixed to the lab that day.

CHAPTER TWELVE

Discovery Clause

It was the day for the discovery motion to be heard before the Motion Judge, who had been assigned to hear all forms of motions for all criminal matters. As the various lawyers straggled into the courtroom and checked in with the court clerk, they were numbered in order of appearance. When the judge arrived, he called the list in order of appearance. By now, my Motion to Suppress had also been filed.

A Motion to Suppress is filed when defense counsel believes the facts demonstrate that some evidence has been obtained by unconstitutional means —illegal search, coerced confession, etc.

When my case was called, the judge postponed the hearing on the Motion to Suppress until the time of trial. This was a frequent but not terribly helpful ruling. If the hearing can be held well before trial and is successful, it may completely dispose of the case by knocking out nearly all necessary evidence to prove a case. Even if unsuccessful, defense counsel can learn an awful lot from the testimony and help him prepare for trial. It can cover some areas of the police testimony that he was not allowed to hear during the preliminary hearing. Most judges, to save time, liked to hear the Motion testimony and, if the Motion was denied and there was to be no jury trial, they would simply incorporate the Motion Testimony into the Trial record and not have to hear it twice. Since juvenile trials were not jury trials unless the DA elected to try the juvenile defendant as an adult, and, since juveniles did not usually face severe sentences, the less time the judge had to spend the better. I could also ask to postpone the trial after the discovery motion was heard if I had a good reason to do so. Also, to spare time, the judge ordered the DA and I to go into a side room and negotiate what items I had asked for in discovery he a) had and would produce b) had and refused to produce or c) didn't have. We went into the room and pulled out my list of requested items. "I don't know how you made up this list, but I have no idea what most of it is," the ADA stated.

"Okay, let's start with simplest first. The Police 49, all prior drafts of the 49, and all police notes."

The ADA was a young thin woman. She was very nervous and had obviously not been doing this for very long. I selected the intimidation approach. I pulled my chin up and tried to look intense.

"All I have is this 49."

"Miss ______."

"Jeffers."

"Ms. Jeffers. That is not good enough. This is time stamped a few days ago and at the preliminary hearing I saw an earlier version. An earlier and possibly different version may be Brady material." Brady material is derived from a case where the government was required to give exculpatory material to the defense counsel—that is all material which might tend to show the defendant was not guilty. A prior statement contradicting a later statement would obviously fling the new 49 version into doubt. "If I find a prior 49 that's different someone's going to jail." That was enough to scare her. She knew I was right. "What efforts did you use to get the early 49 version I asked for?" She knew she was under a strong compulsion by the courts to drill the police on anything I asked for.

"I'll bring them all in and ask them again."

"Now, who is they? Who is this AG agent and who were the other police on this case?"

"All I have is the name on the 49 for the Philadelphia officer. I don't see any reference to the AG."

"Who was the detective or Sargeant on this case?"

"I don't know that either."

"Okay, that's enough. I want this on the record. If I find this stuff later, heads will roll." I stomped out and sat in the courtroom with a scowl on my face. Eventually the judge got through the list, and called our case again.

Eventually the judge looked my way. "Mr Magen. What can we do for you?"

"Your honor, I believe there is information, documents etc., I am being denied access to, especially Brady material, and I want to put my demands (no longer requests) on the record. If something I ask for surfaces, there is at least an appellate issue, at worst…well at worst, some very bad faith." I didn't want to begin making criminal accusations, or push the judge. The words "Prosecutorial Misconduct" was an extremely harsh accusation to make at this stage. Often, screwups within the DA's or police bureaucracies caused lost paper, files or evidence, but those were usually only delays not total losses.

"Very well, Mr. Magen, let's go down your list." "The prior versions of the 49 and the police notes." "Sounds reasonable. Mr Magen."

"I only have the current one I gave to counsel. I told him I'd drill the police for the other documents."

"Your honor, I saw the officer reading from one at the preliminary hearing."

"Very well, Ms. Jeffers. I order you and the police to produce them if they exist."

"Thank you, your honor. I want the names etc of the Attorney General's agent at the scene and any other police officers involved in the planning or execution of the raid or the arrest."

"Fair enough, names of other witnesses are always welcome, Mr. Magen. Ms. Jeffers."

"I don't know that yet, your honor."

"I order you to find out." So far, so good.

"Any DVD's of the bar for the date of the arrest and the prior two weeks."

"I have the DVD of the downstairs area on the night of the arrest." "Your honor, the police officer testified of a relevant confrontation with my witness two weeks prior which he claimed gave him probable cause for the arrest. I know there are two other cameras in the bar, I saw them. I also know this camera records continuously for at least two weeks. I want to see it."

"Fair enough, counsel. Ms. Jeffers?" "We don't have it, your honor."

"Get them. Ms. Jeffers. I'm sensing something unhealthy here." "I hope not, your honor." I now had the judge's full attention and a very good record.

"Next, your honor. I need the names of the two johns, the other prostitute and the bartender on the night of the arrest. Most contemporaneous witnesses, your honor."

"I don't have those names yet. I will ask the police officer." "Good idea, Ms. Jeffers. I would hope so! What else, Mr. Magen?" "The condom, the rape kit, any fingerprints."

"Miss Jeffers?"

"Sorry, your honor. No, no, and no." "Again, Ms. Jeffers. Get them!"

I then ran down a list of totally random, non-existent witnesses names which I had added to the list before. Again, a series of nos from Ms. Jeffers and more orders from the judge.

"Anything else? Mr. Magen."

"Not at this time, your honor. I'm sorry to take up the court's time with this, but I do need those items for my defense."

"Perfectly understandable, Mr. Magen. Ms. Jeffers, I mean what I say. Get them."

"Understood, your honor."

Chapter Thirteen

Meeting with Client

I now had to bring Carmen up to date on what was happening. By now, Carmen had moved totally out of her mother's apartment and in with Roselita. She was going to school with Roselita's daughter. I met her in one of the classrooms of her school. Carmen looked totally different. She was well scrubbed and had on a Catholic school uniform—blue plaid skirt, white blouse, blue cardigan sweater and black shoes with white socks. I will forgive my male readers their impure thoughts here. This iconic uniform is probably at the top of the list of male fantasies. If Carmen had worn this in her previous professional life, I am sure she could have charged at least double. As for me, the ethical constraints of my profession eradicated all such fantasies. I saw a pretty little teeny bopper with a rather intelligent look on her face. After bringing her up to date on everything, I explained to her the offer from Lynch's father—that she would get a portion of the proceeds when the bar was sold.

"I have given this matter a great deal of thought. I don't think I can accept this lawyer's offer. It would amount to blackmail. In Pennsylvania, we do not permit minors to bring suit for sexual abuse to which they gave consent. So we couldn't sue anyone if we wanted to. The only reason then for accepting money would be to withhold evidence, or commit perjury. Since this is a crime, I can't advise you to accept the money. But now, it bumps into question the whole operation of the bar, so I have to ask you some more questions. First, do you know who owned the bar?"

"No."

"Do you know who delivered the drugs?" "I don't know him but I could ID him."

"Do you know Peter Lynch? The curly haired guy lawyer who was there the night of the arrest?"

"No. I had seen him there before, but I never met him." "Could you ID him?"

"Yes, of course."

"Did you know if he owned the bar?" "No. I didn't know that. Is it true?"

"I'm not sure yet. Do you know the bartender's name?"

"I only knew him as Emilio. But he lived just up the street from the bar."

"What did he do at the bar?"

"He served the customers. Sold dope. Took my $35. Drank a bit and chatted with the customers. That was about it."

"Did he have anything to do with you or the other girls?"

"No. He took our $35 and handed us the key. If we were over an hour, he would scold us, but that was about it."

"How many times was Louie there with you?" "Just two. The night of the arrest and once before."

"Did you know the other lady on the night of the arrest?"

"I only knew her as Chiquita. I know that wasn't her real name.
She was from out of town, I think." "Okay. That's about it."

"Okay, one question. If you can't get the money from the sale of the bar, can I do it on my own?"

"It would probably be bribery or obstruction of justice, and it would give you a criminal record. Plus, you don't know what you are doing. You are in a pool with sharks and a pretty little minnow like you could get eaten up. My advice is don't do it."

"I hear you. Now, I have another question. Why are you doing all this and not getting paid?"

"I guess it really interests me. I'm mostly retired, I don't need the money and I smell a rat—a bigger rat than your Louie. There's a coverup going on and I can feel it."

"Are you sure I can't pay you somehow?" "No. No, that's fine. Just do well in school." "Alright, thank you."

I could almost hear the wheels turning inside that pretty little but very street-smart head—maybe too street-smart for her own good.

CHAPTER FOURTEEN

Notes on Thumb Drive

It was time to think things over and put my notes on my computer. By reviewing the facts, I knew my mind would start to formulate a few theories. In addition to my notes, I put photos of all the evidence in the computer record. Then, I put the notes on two thumb drives. I knew some of this information was dangerous and my file in someone else's hands was my insurance policy. Since Carmen was my client, I could give her a thumb drive and the second I gave to my daughter with instructions not to open it unless Carmen died or gave her consent. As in law school, I had to answer the question "who is doing what to whom?"

First, Carmen had been boinked by Judge Bastoncino, a juvenile court judge, who had thus committed Statutory Rape, and I could prove it. The judge's name was being hidden in the investigation by someone. The plot involved at a minimum a Philadelphia cop and some unknown agent from the AG's office. The DA's office was probably not involved and was being hung out to dry by the cops by withholding evidence.

The arrest of Carmen on the night in question was bogus. The police had no search or arrest warrant to enter the room and observe her, the judges, the dope or anything else. Without more, all the evidence would be suppressed. The testimony about the police officer's first contact with Carmen was totally fabricated and, thanks to Liam Lynch, I had the CD of the night in question which proved it. The cop had not only made an obviously bad arrest but made up a bad story. He was in hot water and I could prove it. What struck me was that the actual arrest was so bad, that it seemed like it was never intended to result in a conviction or a trial. Clearly, Carmen was not a target —she could have easily plead guilty and gotten only a minor juvenile probation, but any decent lawyer could have knocked the evidence and the case out completely. Without Carmen in jeopardy, she would not have to rat out the Judge or Peter Lynch to gain immunity. So long as she had an experienced attorney, she had no need to cooperate with the authorities. Perhaps that was the reason that I had been paid—so that a public defender would not ho-hum the case and screw it up.

But something else was going on here. Why should a cop and an AG agent bother to arrest little Carmen and stop there? The arrest may have been intended to trigger a forfeiture of the bar or to blackmail the judge or Peter Lynch. If a crime is committed on a piece of real estate and the owner knows of the crime and permits it to go on, he forfeits the property.

Blackmailing the judge wasn't worth a whole plot. Judges didn't make much money, but got a nice state pension. Judges paid $450,000 to get a cushy job where they didn't have to work hard, couldn't get fired and everyone kissed their ass. They were generally formerly incompetent lawyers. The only reason to blackmail him was to have him decide a case in a particular way. Since he only sat in minor juvenile matters, he never handled anything that important. Besides, it was well known that his election as a judge had been backed by two construction unions and a few guys loosely connected to the South Philly mob. Any one of these could act as his bag man if someone were to fix a case.

A whole expensive blackmail plot was not necessary.

Lynch was a different matter. He might be implicated in the criminal activity of the bar, and his obvious connection through his secretary could easily be proven, so he might lose the bar and the real estate in a forfeiture.

But, since it was not his bar in the first place, it would be no skin off his nose. He would lose face with the client who actually owned the bar, but the client deserved to lose the bar anyway since he not only owned the bar but fostered the prostitution and drug sales. Besides, without the drug sales and prostitution, the bar was not worth that much anyway. A couple hundred thousand—while nice money—was not worth involving a cop and AG agent in a coverup which might threaten both their careers and cost Lynch his ticket as a lawyer.

It had to be something else. Then, I began to wonder just how much the bar made. After all, I was a business lawyer to begin with. Time to ask Carmen some more questions.

I reached Carmen on her cellphone. "Carmen, I've got a few more questions. About what did you make a week?"

"About a thousand after I paid for the room." "How many tricks in a week?"

"Depending on tips and whatnot, between seven and ten a week at about $100 to $200—mostly over $150." Let me see, about eight tricks times 150 was $1200 per week less $280 for the room was about $920 per week per girl. The bar made $280 per week or $15,000 per year per girl. Not a lot of money for a risky criminal operation rife with kickbacks or shakedowns by the cops, difficulties with the girls and many personal management problems as well as lots of easy witnesses.

"How about the drugs. Who delivered them and how much?"

"I saw a Hispanic guy deliver an empty case of beer about once a week of uncut coke and meth. I would guess about a ki."

"Could you ID the delivery guy?" "Sure."

"Did they cut the stuff at the bar?"

"A couple girls would come in and cut the stuff in the basement." "How strong was the stuff?"

"About the same as the street?"

Coke is cut with 10 grams of vitamin B12 to 28 grams of coke (28 grams to an ounce), so a kilogram (1000 grams) becomes 1357 grams. A gram of cut coke goes for about $50 to $100. Let's say a ki when cut and sold at $50-100 has a street value of about $70,000 to $135,000. An uncut kilo from a source would cost about $20,000. Meth has about the same math. (Sorry, couldn't resist.) So, the bar made $48,000 profit a week or over $2,400,000 per year at 2.2 pounds of coke per week.

I was beginning to understand the problem. The bar made a ton of money selling coke and very little with the girls. The prostitution is, obviously, a crime and carries its own risks. Prostitutes are generally not reliable employees and each one and every john is a security risk. Different police are involved in vice, so there is another set of people to pay off. Why jeopardize a business worth two million a year with one that nets $100,000 and carries substantial risk? So the Philadelphia cop had uncovered the prostituion business but not the drug operation. The bar was still open, and the drugs in Carmen's room had not been tied to the bar, as yet.

So someone with a police connection had managed to tip off the cop to raid Carmen, and not to mention Carmen's john in the report. Somehow, the arresting officer never extended his arrest to search for drugs at the bar. Was he tipped off or just incompetent?

Whoever tipped off the cops had to know about the illegal activity at the bar, and want to protect it, but put the bar owner at risk for conducting the prostitution business. After all Carmen could easily ID the bartender whom she paid and implicate the bar owner's agent in the business and thus, get the whole bar shut down.

The bar owner did not want to bring the cops down on his own bar. The bartender probably didn't want to do so either; he had a cushy job handled a lot of money, had a lot of very sensitive information about the bar and, as a result, was probably paid well for his loyalty. So it had to be someone else: another drug dealer, Peter Lynch, or a customer of the bar, each of whom would not wish to jeopardize the drug business, would want to take it over intact.

Carmen had enough information to interfere with those plans. She might be in jeopardy. The present bar owner also might be in trouble as well.

I called up Carmen to warn her of any possible danger. I had to figure my next move; a) talk to Judge Bastoncino, b) talk to Peter Lynch or c) contact Mehle from IAD to see if he came up with anything. I chose the Judge first. I asked for an appointment to see him and explained that I was Carmen's lawyer.

CHAPTER FIFTEEN

Conference with Judge Bastoncino

The conference was set up with the Judge in his chambers at 12:30 just after he recessed court for the day. As I walked in he had two attorneys with him, whom he introduced as representing him. I never liked the Judge and knew he never liked me. I also knew he was stupid, but had acquired great skills at self preservation.

He opened the discussion: "I suppose you are enjoying this." "Judge, as you know I represent the girl you know as Flora. I don't know what you have told your attorneys so I don't know how much to reveal about what I know in front of them."

Joe Lambrusco, a lawyer I knew and respected, spoke up. "Mr. Magen, we have been told everything. Let's hear what you have to say." Although we knew each other well, Joe was addressing me by my last name. He was warning me that we were now adversaries.

"All right then. The judge was copulating with my client Flora, when he was caught in a police raid. Flora is underage. There were cocaine lines on the nightstand table. His name does not appear in the arrest record, as yet, and did not come up in the preliminary hearing or the police 49." Judge Bastoncino exploded. "Are you blackmailing me? I'll have your ticket, you motherfucker…" His additional blustering was cut short by Joe Lambrusco.

Joe held his client's arm and asked "what do you want?"

"Mr. Lambrusco, I think you know I'm not interested in blackmail. The way I figure it, your client and mine are both in some kind of trouble.

Someone tipped two cops—one an AG agent—about the prostitution. It is a totally bogus arrest without a search warrant. Why the bar was in the prostitution game is beyond me. It didn't make much money out of it, but it does a ton in cocaine sales. Someone wants that bar and someone may go after anyone that interferes in the drug sales. So far the bar has not been shut down. But your client and mine know about the drug sales. Either one could put the bar out of business and put some drug dealers in jail. If we can do that, we might be in big trouble. Also, my client can rat out yours and get immunity. Your client can rat out Peter Lynch who took him to the bar. Lynch may be the one who wants the bar for himself or a partner, as I figure it."

The judge was shifting in his seat and about to burst out again. Lambrusco seemed to follow where I was going. "OK, Mr. Magen. What do you want?"

"Information. Reliable information from your client off the record that may protect my client."

"How do I know you won't blackmail us?"

"First, the judge doesn't have much money. He doesn't sit on big enough cases for anyone to go to the trouble. Anyone who wants him can find a bag man for a lot cheaper."

Again, Bastoncino exploded. "Bag man… Bag man… you nasty son of a bitch!" Again, Lambrusco put the hand on his shoulder.

"What bag man?"

"His campaign contributors, outside of family, were limited to two union members and some mob wannabes. We could probably get him for the level of case he handles for a few cheesesteaks in the right place." I was beginning to enjoy this, but I did have a goal here and I didn't want to lose sight of the goal.

Again, the judge blew up, Lambrusco proceeded cautiously. "What proof do you have?"

"First, to ensure my own safety, I put all my notes and photos on f lash drives and gave them to someone to give out if Flora or I are injured or killed.

"Second, I got the judge's DNA on his cigar and bar glass from Springbrook Golf Club on May 2 and have them safely stored with the affidavit from a detective. Incidentally, he was playing with three lawyers who appeared in his court the following week. He did not pick up the tab for his golf, lunch, beer or cigar, as is his well known custom. He was wearing red plaid shorts and a red shirt. The rest of the evidence will have to remain confidential." A brief whispering session between Lambrusco and Bastincino ensued.

"Okay, what do you want to know?"

"First, what is his relationship to Peter Lynch and what can you tell me about that night?" Another whispering session.

"Are we off the record?"

"Absolutely. I'm not a cop and I'm not blackmailing you, and I'm not wired."

"Lynch used to take other lawyers and judges to the bar for some action with the girls. I never knew Flora was underage. Lynch seemed to know everyone there including the bartender."

"Did Lynch do any coke?" "I don't know."

"Did you?"

"None of your business."

"Okay, we'll come back to that. How is it that you weren't arrested or named in the report?"

"Lynch was on the phone with someone during the arrest. I don't know what he said. He told me not to worry. I was pretty shook up. They led Flora off after she got dressed and I walked out with Lynch. And that was the end of that."

"Did you do any more investigation of your own?" "No. Lynch said it was taken care of."

"Did you do anything specific to get Lynch to invite you to the bar?" "What do you mean?"

"Come on, judge. Give me a break."

"OK. No. Lynch was doing a favor for somebody else. He never appears in front of me. One of my friends was just doing me a favor."

"Do you know who got you the invite?"

"No. It could have been a number of people. Lynch must do this a lot."

"How many times have you been there?" "Three."

"I have to tell you there were a number of cameras in the bar. You probably appeared more than one time for your visits."

"Oh, shit. I'm fucked."

"Now now calm down. You haven't been arrested or blackmailed yet. You don't have any real money. You were probably not the target, just incidental. No one has interviewed Flora, and we probably won't need immunity if I suppress the arrest and raid. Has anyone contacted you about anything yet?"

"No."

"Did you know either of the cops on the raid?"

"No."

"Are you sure? No court cases, no nothing? Do you think they were at all interested in you?"

"Well, pretty sure."

"So you might be home free."

"You're not saying anything."

"I don't think I could do anything without implicating my client."

"So there's nothing you want from me."

"No. Just this information. Oh yes. When I'm in your courtroom you could kiss my ass."

The judge looked back and forth between me and Lambrusco with a worried look. Lambrusco broke into a big smile. "Very funny, Magen. Very funny."

We got up to leave. That went well. It was pretty obvious the cops were told to do something specific and that they were wired. I was getting a bad feeling about Peter Lynch.

CHAPTER SIXTEEN

Call from Carmen re: $100K

"**M**r. Magen, I'm sorry to bother you. You've done so much already."

"Is that you, Carmen?"

"Yes. I have a new question. Roselita and I may inherit some money from a relative in Honduras and we want to know what to do with it."

"How much are we talking about?" "Over $100,000."

"U.S. dollars." "Yes."

I didn't claim to be a financial expert but a number of things were pretty obvious to me. The stock market was a jungle for people like Carmen and she would be ripped off in no time. Mutual funds or bonds were usually good, but these were very iffy times and I just didn't trust the economy. These so-called "safe investments" weren't so safe anymore. I really knew the best investment for them under these circumstances, I thought it would be a no-brainer. She should buy a house, possibly even a duplex in a nice neighborhood in the northeast and move there with Roselita, her cousin and herself. Over the long haul, a personal residence was the best investment for most people.

I explained this to Carmen. Then, I referred her to a client of mine who was a realtor in the northeast. In Philadelphia, the northeast area was developed after World War II and had a vast number of very sturdy new houses, twin, duplexes et al which represented a good value for the blue collar community. You had to choose your neighborhood well—schools, crime, transportation etc were all considerations, but I knew Bella Antimov would know how to get the best house for the money and weave them through the process seamlessly. When I called Bella, she offered to kick back 1% of the 3% of her agent's commission to me. I told Carmen all about the problems of buying a house, and my 1% kickback. She was overjoyed with the prospect and seemed happy I would add the 1% to my legal fee.

Bella was a Russian jew who had come out of Kiev in the early 1990s and left her husband behind. Her English was good and she had a great business sense. Although she had an engineering degree from a Ukrainian university, she enjoyed the action of wheeling and dealing in real estate more. She was always impeccably dressed and knew the northeast like the back of her hand. I knew she would find the perfect house for Carmen and Roselita.

CHAPTER SEVENTEEN

Call from Bastoncino

My cell phone jingled on the fifth hole. It is always bad form to talk on your cell phone on the gold course, so I shut off the call and turned it off. By the ninth hole, I took a look at my messages. This was like the old days, before I retired. There were five messages from the same number—a city exchange. Again, I turned the phone off.

At the end of 18, I checked the messages again. Now there were nine, all from the same city number. I called it. The next thing I heard was a blast from Bastoncino.

"You bastard, you motherfucker. How could you do that?" On and on. "Yes Judge, what's the problem?" Personally enjoying every delicious moment.

"I got the flash drive handed to me and a telephone call. I'm being blackmailed. And you promised, you motherfucker, you bastard…"

"Whoa, whoa. I don't know what you're talking about. Who is doing this?"

"I don't know but it must be you."

"No. I don't know anything about it. How did this happen?" "Some Spanish guy handed me a package. It had the f lash drive and a note. The letters were cut out from a magazine. The drive had pictures of the bar, Carmen, the declarative affidavit, the DNA results—I'm fucked. How could you do this?"

"I didn't do anything. What does the note say?"

"They want $100,000 in cash and they want me to resign from the bench."

"Whoa! I did not do this. I made a few flashdrives and told certain people to hold them for safekeeping. That's all. I don't want your $100,000."

"Well, they want me to deliver it in exchange for the f lash drive." "I don't even know who they are."

"It's blackmail. I won't pay. I'll call the cops. I'll get the bastards." "If that's what you want. I have nothing to do with it."

"How about your client. Did she do this?" "A sixteen year old prostitute. I doubt it."

"Maybe she had help. I only know her aunt, an older lady who hardly speaks English. I doubt it was her."

"I find out and I'll get them. I swear it. You can tell everyone. I mean it." While it was great fun to have that sleazy bastard twisting in the wind, I was more than curious as to how my f lashdrive had ended up in his hands. Was Carmen that smart?

CHAPTER EIGHTEEN

Liam Lynch Second Call

"David, glad I could catch you in."

"Ah Liam, how is everything?"

"Well, I've given my son a good talking to about jeopardizing the firm. He seems to understand. And I'm very grateful to you."

"What for, Liam?"

After a short pause. "Yes, yes, I understand. I'm most grateful."

"But I…"

"Some man called and agreed to accept an offer for Flora and I'm most grateful. It gives us some peace of mind."

"But I… Your son seemed particularly angry at me for something."

"I think that must have been before we talked. I think he's turned around now."

"Good to hear it, Liam."

That call was a total mystery. I never accepted any deal with Liam but he seemed to think I had. Peter Lynch certainly didn't think so. I certainly felt things were going on out of my control. First the judge and now Liam. Who else knew? Carmen?

CHAPTER NINETEEN

Lambrusco Call

It wasn't that long after my call with the judge that his attorney Joe Lambrusco called. Now, he was on a first name basis.

"Hello, David. I just heard about the blackmail to our friend Judge Bastoncino."

"I got a few thousand well-chosen swear words myself."

"I have to know what's going on. You promised you were not interested in squeezing the good judge."

"I'm not. I have nothing to do with this. I certainly don't want the judge's money. Although I bet he has a good stash. He hasn't picked up a check in the fourteen years since he became a judge."

"Now, now, let's be nice. Who do you think is involved?"

"I gave out a few flash drives to a number of people in case anything happened to me. My guess is that someone got hold of the f lash drive and saw it for a few bucks."

"But why do they want him to resign as judge?"

"I'd guess that it's either something personal or they don't like judges of juvenile court fucking underage prostitutes."

"Something personal, you guess."

"Surely, you must know some people who hate the judge enough to want his hide."

"He certainly was not well liked." "You think!"

"Now, now, let's be nice. Could this be your client?"

"She got a f lash drive. But I don't think she is smart enough or brave enough or savvy enough to take down a judge."

"Maybe, she has some help."

"Maybe. But I've been thinking. This thing may blow up further. I reported the coverup by the cops to IAD. The bar was doing a lot of coke sales—far more in value than the prostitution business. If this business blows up and your client appears in the bar's CD, which someone must have, he's in for a much bigger hurt than a little blackmail. He'd be in the papers as well as losing a few bucks. If he resigns, he keeps his reputation and can be an arbitrator or something without losing his license. I promised that Carmen will not testify in a stat rape charge, so the criminal case goes away."

"Yeah, I see that. He resigns, drops a few bucks, and disappears, but keeps his license, and, by the way, his pension. It's something to think about. I'll get back to you."

It was just after 2:00 a.m. when the bars by law closed and the patrons had finished their last call. More vigilant than the Liquor Control Board were the bartenders who had been on their feet since 6:00 p.m. and wanted to go home. The bar flies trundled out as the bartenders swabbed the bar, put up some of the chairs on the tables and turned out the lights. The men ambled down the street to Ms. Mae's who sold 40s so the men could go across the street to the empty parking lot and drink. It was a nice night, moonlit, clear.

A sleek black Escalade cruised down 5th Street, and Juan Diaz settled in the passenger seat. He had made his way from the Dominican Republic years ago, fought his way through the Puertoricanos who mocked his Dominican accent. He was going to learn English and be somebody. So at 14, when he was recruited to run drugs to the street dealers and pick up their cash, he kept his eyes and ears open. His mother never knew the stash he was collecting. While the other boys hung out, chased girls and smoked dope, he grew his stash. He was never attractive to the women and never tried. He could buy them when he wanted. He got the boss to let him manage a corner. Then, he used his stash to buy a few bricks and he got his own dealer to sell out of a house. He was at the crucial point where he had clout and could buy in large chunks wholesale and bagged and cut to be sold retail. He was somebody. Although he was short and squat with no neck and acne scars, he commanded respect. So he drove through his neighborhood staring out the heavily tinted windows as Julio drove. Both held their Glocks on their laps. It was late and anything could happen. They drove up to Tito's. Juan got out his keys, shook the key ring and jumped out of the SUV and went to the rear door while Julio, tall and dark, stayed watch at the sidewalk. Juan went to the safe on the first floor. It was a drop safe. The bartenders put their paperwork and receipts into a trap door and the contents fell to the bottom out of their reach. Only Juan had the combo. He opened the side door to the basement and scraped the wrapped bills and paperwork into a gym bag and slammed the safe shut. He climbed the stairs and exited to the alley where Julio waited. Juan waved his gun and he and Julio got back in the Escalade. He was now $20,000 richer.

The SUV rolled smoothly to a stop two lights down. Then out of nowhere a utility van swung in front of the SUV, blocking it while a Chrysler 300 pulled up beside Juan's window. Shots rang out of the driver's and rear windows at Juan and Julio who slumped in the front seats. Two men jumped out, shot open the passenger door of the Escalade and grabbed Juan's gym bag. They jumped back into the Chrysler and took off east. The utility van lumbered off south. The men drinking 40s ran for cover. A purple Mustang with two white stripes cruised off to the west. And then there was silence. A few lights turned on in the second floors of some of the houses. In a few minutes, three police cars sped up with sirens blasting. They saw a sleek black Escalade with two men slumped in the front seat with its lights on and both dead. The senior officer radioed into the station house. It was not until daylight that the forensics team and the coroner would be there. In the meantime, police yellow tape was wrapped around the Escalade and traffic cones directed cars around the crime scene. No witnesses would come forward.

The forensics people ran around taking pictures. The coroner's men heaved the bodies into their van. This was an easy report: clear gun shots to the head, about 2:00 a.m. Gunshots at passenger door. No brass on the street. A clean assassination. The police tape was removed. The morning traffic resumed. All was quiet again until a few cars by in the early morning.

CHAPTER TWENTY

Telephone Call with Peter Lynch

I hadn't ever talked with Peter Lynch although I knew his father Liam well.

It was about time I filled in a few blanks with him to see where he stood. So I called.

"Peter Lynch."

"Speaking."

"Peter, this is David Magen. I spoke with your father about the situation at Tito's. I understand you know of my involvement with Flora."

"Yes, Mr. Magen." Uh, oh, "Mr. Magen" it was going to be. "I know Carmen's involvement." Another uh oh, he was assuring me he knew Carmen's real name and probable whereabouts. It didn't sound like he distanced himself from the bar very much.

"Okay. Let's get down to it. Your father wanted to pay us to keep your name out of the investigation and I turned him down. I don't do blackmail. I'm interested in my client's safety."

"So what the hell do you want from me?" No longer an uh, oh— outright hostility. "My father should not have spoken to you. I can protect my interests and those of my secretary without your help. I don't need you sniffing around." Okay, so no more nice luncheons at his club. I got that.

One more attempt. "Look I've known your father a long time. He knows I'm a straight shooter. Let…"

"Well, I'm not my father."

"Look, I don't want your money."

"Yeah, I'm sure. Just leave me alone."

That was interesting. What did it mean? He must have known Carmen knew about the drug deliveries. He also knew Carmen knew he brought the judge to the bar. He probably had been called by the judge about someone's blackmail. If he hadn't, he would be. So far the bar's license was not in trouble, but Carmen could create enough problems if she cooperated with the D.A., but she hadn't done that yet and probably would not have to in order to get her charges dropped. What was Peter so mad about? Maybe he was being blackmailed, maybe his client had a fight with him about the raid and they were trying to figure out what to do."

Let me see. Peter's secretary was the title owner of the bar, for Peter's client —the drug dealer, who because of his prior criminal record could not own the bar. The client was making a pot of money out of the bar. Peter had to have told him the liquor license might be in jeopardy because of the raid. So far there had been no notice that the license might be in jeopardy. If so, the whole drug operation might be in trouble. Peter might be able to keep a lid on an investigation into the bar or he might not. In any case, the drug dealer would owe him big time for getting the bar out of trouble. No one knew who the real owner was except Peter and the bartender, for sure. If he was the guy who delivered the drugs, Carmen might be able to ID him.

On the other hand, maybe another drug dealer wanted the bar shut down so that he could pick up the drug sales in the Hispanic neighborhood. Maybe, he alerted the cops. But if he did, why not have them raid for drugs instead of just prostitution?

On the other hand, how did Peter and the judge avoid getting named in the police reports?

CHAPTER TWENTY-ONE

Death of Dealer

I was reading the Sunday papers with my wife. Usually a pleasant quiet time over bagels, cream cheese and Nova. A few dabs at the Sunday New York Times puzzle and then off to golf. When I got to the local news section, there was a story about a Black Escalade being ambushed that night near Tito's bar. Usually the paper had a few Friday or Saturday dustups with a few people getting shot. There were even a few drive-by shootings. Probably, some tiffs between low level drug dealers over turf, or some lover's quarrels. The Black Escalade however made it a bigger story. It was definitely a drug assassination at a high level. On my way out to the golf club, it even made the radio news segment. Then, I got a call from Roselita.

"Meester Magen, Carmen she go into hide. She gone." Then a few more jumbled sentences.

"Wait, Roselita. Let me get my daughter." I was able to catch my daughter home playing with my grandson.

"Sweet Pea, let me ring you in on a three way with Roselita."

I rang Sweet Pea aka Leslie in on the call, and listened to several volleys back and forth. Finally Leslie spoke English.

"Dad, this Carmen has something to do with the shooting last night. She left the house and went to hide with friends in New Jersey. She'll call you and let you know where she is. Roselita also said she loves the new house. I couldn't understand what she meant about that. But Carmen will call you. Did you get all that?"

"Yes. I did. And very strange. I hope she didn't kill someone."

"No, I don't get that out of what Roselita said, but somehow she is involved."

"Okay, then I just wait."

"That's what it seems like."

CHAPTER TWENTY-TWO

Iwas dozing off about 11PM on Sunday when the phone rang. "Mr. Magen, is that you?"

"Yes, Carmen. Where are you? No, wait, don't tell me yet. What's happened?"

"Remember the other girl?"

"I never met her. I thought she disappeared."

"Well, she told me to disappear myself. The boss got himself killed." "What does that have to do with you?"

"I think I know too much. Emilio wouldn't say, but he said whoever was after the boss could be after me. He told me to keep my mouth shut and hide. Too much was leaking out."

"So you think your boss may have been killed over something at the bar."

"Probably, but the boss had been antsy ever since the raid. He didn't like it and told me to stay away. I think he's the one who sent you the $2,000 to help with my arrest and keep me on his side."

"His side. Were there any other people involved with the bar?" "I know Emilio, of course. And the guy who delivered the beer

boxes with the coke. Oh…and I knew the guy with curly hair in the Lincoln. He was the owner's lawyer and got comped at the bar."

"That's all your guess." "That's all I can think of."

It was probably a good time to ask her about the call from Liam and the judge about the blackmail. One of the things a lawyer learns is not to ask your client too much about what they do. It is very easy to become an accessory. If I heard she was blackmailing someone, I could not let her lie about it if I knew. I could not suborn perjury. On the other hand, I had to maintain confidentiality on anything I learned; but I could not advise her to lie to law enforcement. I could tell her not to speak at all and conceal a possible crime. I was a lawyer not a social worker, or a police officer. Most of the public never understood this rather difficult role, but it is necessary to maintain an adversarial legal system. The correct action was to avoid knowing, not to lie to the police and to tell the client to insist on her right not to incriminate herself. Besides, if I spoke to her in person, I would know without knowing. "Carmen, we'll have to meet so we can talk privately. I don't like the phones. I want to see you about 6PM tomorrow. Let's say at the AW Root Beer Stand on Route 73." That way I could see in all directions on a busy highway and not be bugged.

"Fine. See you then."

CHAPTER TWENTY-THREE

Carmen at the A and W

I parked across the street from the A and W and crossed over the eight lanes of Route 73 and tried to see if anyone was waiting to see us. It looked pretty good. Carmen stepped out of an old SUV and sat on one of the outer benches. I walked over and sat across from her. She ordered a double root beer f loat and two hot dogs. I will never know where she puts it all.

"Carmen, where are you staying?"

"Here, I wrote it on a scrap of paper. By the way, I feel terrible that you are doing all this work and I haven't paid you."

"No. That's fine. I'm really enjoying all this. Besides, I made enough money long ago. This is a great adventure. Unless you get hurt."

"No I'm fine. There are lots of latinos in Deptford and I fit right in. I stay with my uncle. He's a very smart guy."

"Carmen, did he visit the judge?"

This question threw her for a loop. "I don't know." Good, she was playing the game. I would never know.

"Well, if he had visited the judge or Peter Lynch, he could be traced to you." It was out there. I knew. She knew I knew, and she knew not to show she knew I knew. Got it. Not bad for a sixteen year old weighing less than 90 pounds packing away enough calories to sustain a nose tackle. She had ordered another milkshake and two more hot dogs. "If he can be traced or followed, he could be in trouble and so could you."

"No. He's been a drug courier and spent time in the slammer. When he got enough money, he started his own body shop. He restores old cars, and raises his kids. He's no dummy. He also says you're great and I should do everything you say."

"Ah. Good advice. By the way, did you look at any houses?"

"We found a duplex in the northeast. Just right. Three bedrooms up and two down in a nice neighborhood just off the boulevard. I'll live with Roselita and her daughter and have my own bedroom. I can go to Father Judge if I pass the test."

"Perfect." Father Judge was one of the better parochial schools in the city. Now, all I had to do was keep Carmen from getting killed. At least, I knew the blackmail money was being put to good use.

CHAPTER TWENTY-FOUR

Meeting with Mehle and Homicide

"Mr. Magen. I have to see you." It was Lt. Mehle from Internal Affairs. Maybe, he had something for me about the raid and the two cops. After all my client was still facing trial. I arranged to meet him at IAD headquarters— an island unto itself in the northeast. When I got back to his office, he was sitting there with a homicide detective. Since I had not expected to have anyone else present, I was immediately put on guard. I knew this meeting might be recorded and was to be used to get information from me rather than getting information from Mehle on the two cops who arrested Carmen. Carmen was still facing a trial and possible conviction although that risk was small, I was still her attorney and was bound by attorney-client privilege on anything I knew. I knew the two detectives would play me for a reaction to whatever was discussed.

At this point, Carmen was still a witness with limited credibility who alone could not support any prosecution. Whatever they got, if anything, from her or her attorney would just aid them in further investigation of this murder. I would have to find out what the homicide detective or Lt. Mehle knew and see how valuable Carmen's or my information might be.

I knew starting off on a friendly but professional basis was best. "Gentlemen, I didn't expect you both."

Lt. Mehle was usually direct with people and did not have a reputation for being devious. "Mr. Magen, this is Sgt. McCready from homicide. He is here because I felt you might be able to help us on the Diaz murder."

"Hello, Sargeant. I don't yet know the name of the deceased. Which murder is this?"

"Nice to meet you, Mr. Magen. This is the murder of Juan Diaz 5800 Rising Sun Avenue. The newspapers are calling it the ambush of the Black Escalade. Mr. Diaz and another man were shot in a driveby about 2 AM on Sunday. It certainly appears to be drug-related, over turf or something like that."

"I've certainly heard of that one."

Lt. Mehle began. "Mr. Magen. You asked me about the raid at Tito's Bar by the Philadelphia policeman and the AG agent in which your client was arrested. I spoke to Officer Martin who told me at first that the AG agent was along as an 'observer.' It eventually turned out that he was the informant and was in fact helping in the raid. The failure of the Philadelphia officer to include the AG agent in the report was at the request of the AG agent. Since they often conceal this information for intelligence purposes and to conceal other ongoing investigations, I took him at his word. Until now. Since you shed some light on this and believed that other identities were also concealed possibly for other purposes, I have not closed the matter.

"I should also not say this, but in my investigation, our drug people have been suspicious that drugs were peddled out of Tito's. It may be that Ms. Jacinto knows something about this."

"Uh-huh. Well, as you know my client is still charged with prostitution and drugs. I certainly don't want to jeopardize her status. That is of course my first concern."

Sgt. McCready spoke up. "We both know that it was a bogus arrest. No probable cause. You'll beat that easily."

"No doubt. But I don't want to get her any deeper if what she may have to say could hurt her. At a minimum, I'd need the charges dropped and a letter of immunity local, state and federal."

"No sweat." Sgt. McCready could smell better information. "I'll have that this afternoon."

"Now, Ms. Jacinto may be in danger as a witness to certain facts or events. I need some protection for her."

"Done."

I knew I had these guys' full attention. The next step would be for me to make an "attorney proffer." In this, without giving any real information, not being under oath, and not being held to the truth or falsity, of what I might disclose, I would outline what I knew without any concrete facts or identities. If they liked the shape of the story I told, they would give my client immunity and protection if she told the truth, did not attempt to hide anybody or withhold important facts, and did not commit any new crimes after the deal was made.

The way immunity is played, once offered, works two ways. There is "use" immunity and "transactional" immunity. In the first, the government promises not to "use" the information you provide against you, but if they can in the future, or could have, by other means, prove that you committed a crime they can still prosecute you for it. "Transactional" immunity absolves you of any crime you admit to during questioning up until that point. You get a totally clean slate for all past offenses.

"Get those letters started then and prepare them for this afternoon. I think you'll like what you hear."

Sargeant McCready got up and began speaking on his cell phone in the next room. Meanwhile, I asked Lt. Mehle.

"Did the local cop tell you who the two johns were?"

"No. He said the AG agent said they were cooperating and their ID's had to remain confidential."

"Uh huh. Deeper and deeper. How about the bar's CD from the camera?"

"He claims he didn't know about them." "And the bartender?"

"Never interviewed, never arrested."

"Did you talk to the AG agent or his boss?" "No. They claimed it's out of my jurisdiction."

"How about the condom, the DNA, the rape kit?"

"Apparently, the AG agent intercepted all that and has it for 'further investigation purposes.'"

"And the Philly cop bought that."

"He apparently was very willing to do so." "Didn't he realize what trouble he could get into?"

"I think he felt that a bad arrest on a juvenile for a vice crime would never get noticed."

"But now, we have a homicide. I think he'll be a bit more forthcoming now."

"No doubt."

Sgt. McCready had re-joined us in the middle of the conversation. "Gentlemen. We have a deal if you can help me with the murder case. The letters are being typed as we speak."

It was my turn now. I would have to produce a narration that gave them what they needed but concealed what needed to be concealed and let Carmen tell the details by herself this afternoon.

"When Carmen came to me, she had been arrested for prostitution by two cops in plain clothes. At Tito's Bar, she was working as a prostitute and made coke available to her johns. Each time she needed a room for the encounter, she paid the bartender $35 for the room key and kept the rest herself. She also paid for a bundle of coke bags and made a profit selling it to the john for him to use with her.

"Her payment of the $35 to the bartender makes the room hers for the session. To enter the cop would have needed a warrant which he didn't have.

"He lied when he told about a previous session with her. I have a CD from the bar's camera to prove it.

"So we know the cop is at least a little bit dirty.

"Ms. Jacinto was there with a prominent member of the bar whose name for the time being will be withheld. He was at least guilty of stat rape. I think you will feel when you hear his name that he was a much more important perp than Ms. Jacinto but his name was left out of the report. The cop saw Ms. Jacinto's ID showing she was a minor.

"There was a second girl and a second john who were caught that night. The second girl is nowhere to be found, but could be a good witness. I don't think she was a minor. Her john was another lawyer, whose name will again be withheld, who was 'treating' Ms. Jacinto's john to a freebie. He had some arrangement with the bar that gave him freebies and on a frequent basis, took guests there for a romp in the hay.

"I have some very good information on who he is and what his role in the bar is."

At this point, Sgt. McCready interrupted. "We are very interested in that. We need that information as soon as possible."

"I'll let you know this afternoon when I have all the papers signed.

No huggie, no kissie, till I get a wedding ring." "Very funny. It better be good."

"Somehow, someone had wired the cops to make the arrest, but told them to let the johns, and the bartender go. I suspect it was someone in the AG's office and that the Philly cop was just under his control. He was just not smart enough at the preliminary hearing and Ms. Jacinto thinks the AG guy was in charge.

"Ms. Jacinto can also tell you about regular deliveries of coke to the bartender, can describe the guy who made the delivery and can ID his vehicle. We believe the delivery guy was this Juan Diaz. The bar is dirty but was not touched in the arrest.

"I believe someone may have blackmailed the two johns. I do not know this for a fact, but Ms. Jacinto may be involved. I have received offers to pay us off for her silence, but I have refused both offers. She may have accepted. I will need full immunity for that for her."

I knew most of this would come out from Carmen. It was now time to consider whether to reveal what I knew about the ownership of the bar. This was the vital connection McCready needed for the murder investigation. There was certainly some information they could easily get themselves, I had to at least give them that.

"Another thing you should know: the bar is owned in the name of a secretary of the Lynch law firm. They do extensive liquor law work. The secretary is a show pony for the real owner. It is not legal for a show pony to be the owner; Liquor Control Board rules requires that the holder of a liquor license fully disclose any interest in the bar including financing etc. Convicted felons or those in law enforcement may not own or have an interest in bars. Someone else is the real owner of the bar. I believe I know who the real owner is, and believe this has a great deal to do with your murder investigation.

"Get those letters. I'll get Carmen and you'll get the full story this afternoon.

"Oh, and one more thing. Carmen is just sixteen years old. She needs two more years of high school. If as part of the witness protection you could put her in a catholic girl's boarding school out of the city, I would appreciate it." Lt. Mehle and Sgt. McCready had sat furiously taking notes as I spoke.

When they finally finished their scribbling, they looked up with big smiles. Sgt. McCready said. "You deliver, we deliver."

CHAPTER TWENTY-FIVE

Carmen's Shopping Trip Pre-School

Carmen's acceptance into a witness protection program was received with, at first, great enthusiasm. Her Aunt Roselita was happy to see Carmen's ability to rise above her mother's lifestyle and become something in America. Carmen was not so happy. She was afraid that these girls in some hoity-toity private boarding school would embarrass her and treat her like something from the lower classes. Her English was not refined and she still had a lingering Spanish accent however slight.

At dinner, my wife and daughter now hung on my every word about Carmen and were fascinated by the story. My daughter, Sweet Pea, had one solution. "Shopping."

"Yes, Dad, one of the first things these girls will see is her clothes. She has to fit in. I'll have to inspect her wardrobe."

My little effort at pro bono representation was making the firm a few bucks, so I figured I'd take my wife and daughter out to brunch with Carmen, get them all acquainted and let them go out shopping. I have to say that my wife would be no help. Her usual dress each day consisted of black jeans and a turtle neck. She was not pretentious for which I was eternally grateful and only reluctantly agreed to go shopping with my daughter who enjoyed dressing her. My wife was along on this shopping trip to curb excesses. But they were each excited at the opportunity to dress up their new little doll.

So we went for lunch at a Jewish deli – my daughter's choice – with Carmen. The food was new to her so she took my daughter's advice. As the waitress listened to her order not only a corned beef special, but also a liver knish, and a sampling of whitefish all to be washed down with an authentic New York style egg cream. My wife's raised eyebrows at me, but I could only shrug knowingly. My wife and daughter ordered their usual favorites – white fish on a toasted bagel. I could smell the pastrami on the way in and could not avoid that on rye with a Dr. Brown black cherry.

My girls were anxious to get to know Carmen, this voyager from a foreign lifestyle. Carmen enjoyed the attention as if she was a visitor from another planet willing to shock my women. Fortunately, they did not know about the prostitution part. That would have been too much.

They asked Carmen about her present wardrobe and it was meager.

"I got three thongs."

"Any underwear."

"No. Just thongs, I like them. I wash one out every night."

"How about bras."

"I don't have any. I just wear undershirts if it's cold. I got three of them and I got a couple sports bras."

"Do you know what size you are?"

"Just a little handful."

"How about jeans, and shorts and sneakers?"

"I usually borrow from Roselita's daughter, my cousin. Mostly I got slutty stuff."

"So we need the works for these girls at the private school."

"I guess so." My daughter was going to private school but a Quaker one, not a Catholic one. She figured the Catholic girls were like those from Notre Dame Academy, maybe overly preppy, while her school was retro hippy Bohemian.

So I dropped them off at Ross in Franklin Mills with my credit card and went to the bookstore and sporting goods to browse. I gave them an hour and a half.

As I sat on the bench by the parking lot, I saw my women beaming as they strolled down the sidewalk laden with bundles. Carmen pulled a rolling duffel bag which looked stuffed and was wearing jeans, pre-ripped at the knee and pre-faded, sneakers, and a pink Phillies T shirt and baseball cap. Her hair by now had gone back over the tattoo on the part of her head that had been shaved. As I had feared, my wife and my daughter both had bags they were lugging as well. I knew better than to ask, but I was sure to get a fashion show at home.

"So, Carmen, how did you make out?"

"Mr. Stern, I never had so many clothes. They only wear uniforms at the school, so I don't know if I can wear them all."

Somehow, I knew she would.

I drove Carmen back to her duplex in the Northeast and the rest of us home. I was sure everyone had a wonderful time.

CHAPTER TWENTY-SIX

Carmen at IAD

I returned to IAD with Carmen. I had picked her up after school at the nearest bus stop on the boulevard. I was always amazed at the transformation she could make when I saw her in her school uniform; blue plaid skirt, white blouse, blue cardigan sweater and black flat shoes with white socks. Apparently, the nuns had acquiesced in allowing the girls to wear eye makeup. But even now, Carmen had just a touch of mascara—nothing more. The cops were gonna love her.

Once inside IAD, we were ushered back inside to the same office as before, but this time there was another officer—a Sgt. Jones—a small thin black man in plain clothes. He was from the Drug Unit and was working with homicide on this one.

I had instructed Carmen carefully on being a witness. There were rules. First, tell the truth, don't make things up or elaborate beyond what you know. Second, just answer the question that's asked, don't elaborate, don't get into theories or speculation on the evidence and what it means.

Carmen was very good. She never tried to ID the second john but described his car. She told them she did not know the name of her john until we saw him at Juvenile Court and I told her. She only told what she actually saw or heard.

As I expected, the cops were impressed. They went over and over her story, trying to get more details or tracing out any inconsistencies or contradictions. They were especially concerned about the bartender, and the man who made the deliveries in the beer boxes. Then they brought out some photos. She easily ID'ed Peter Lynch as the second john, Emilio the bartender, and the delivery guy as Juan Diaz. As I suspected, he was one of the two men killed in the Black Escalade.

She also ID'ed the judge as Bastoncino. When she was shown the picture and she named him "Louie," the homicide cop said that the judge had already resigned from the bench, but in secret, and was cooperating with the police for a grant of full immunity. I almost felt sorry for him—although he was a horrible judge, a scumbag and a nasty prick to most of the lawyers, he had come up the hard way. But in the end, his stat rape charge would never see the light of day and he saved his pension. He could still strut around like he was somebody, he just would have to pick up his own tab from now on. They never mentioned any blackmail or extortion on Carmen's part. This was a good sleeping dog to let lie. I hoped she enjoyed her duplex in the northeast.

They also never mentioned any payoffs to Carmen from either Liam or Peter Lynch, but then they had not interviewed them yet. I would cross that bridge later.

After going over her story ad nauseam, the three cops seemed to have exhausted every possible angle. They slid the immunity letter across the table for us to sign. It was in order as I expected. They then slid a witness protection agreement across the table. It was also in order. Apparently, Carmen would be going to boarding school for remedial summer school in Scranton, and if she passed everything, the school would admit her on a scholarship. Carmen had been dipped in shit, but come up smelling like a rose.

I then volunteered a bit of information. I described how the bar had been placed in the name of the Lynch law firm's secretary: how that was money laundering, and a violation of PA liquor laws if the real or part owner was a convicted felon hiding his drug money. I also told them I believed Peter Lynch was making a nice fee for setting up the title this way. I suspected that the deceased drug dealer was the hidden owner, especially since he was the one who made the drug deliveries.

The cops ate that up. I then posed a couple of scenarios. Some rival dealer shot up the decedent and was attempting to take over his territory which included the bar. The vice arrest without the drug raid was targeted to shut down the prostitution trade as a warning shot, or a threat in possible negotiations. A full blown drug raid would have caused the Liquor Control

Board to shut down the bar. Someone wanted the cops to have the bar remain open and not lose its license. Someone was wired to the Philly cop and the AG agent to limit their arrest accordingly. I suspected that Peter Lynch was either going to sell the bar or join in a partnership with this other drug dealer. This whole risky conspiracy was justified by the huge amount of drug sales at the bar.

They seemed to like my idea, but were noncommittal. I guessed I would have to wait to hear what happened in the papers.

Carmen was very happy. She however, seemed to enjoy poking fun at my car, which she seemed to like. But it was, let's say vintage, an oldie. She laughed at the chipped paint and the occasional scrape and the rips here and there in the leather. She asked what color I would like it to be. I told her I had always liked metallic red. That seemed to keep her quiet. I knew she was expecting me to treat her to dinner at the Red Lobster on the boulevard, but I had to get home for dinner. It had been a good day.

Chapter Twenty-Seven

Vacation

Things looked great just as it was time for our vacation. It was great weather in Hilton Head and the time was ripe for golf. My wife and I took off and spent a pleasant week with no cares. Not one call on my cell phone interrupted my mood. When we returned at the end of the week, I was completely refreshed. As we pulled into my driveway, I saw a peculiar car in my familiar spot. It was a dazzling dark metallic red 2002 Thunderbird. My wife began to giggle as my eyes bugged out. After unloading the cab, I ran over to this car. Inside the shabby leather seats had been redone in a deep maroon leather. Of course, the car had been expertly detailed. Astounded, I tried my key in the door and, lo!, it worked. This was my comfortably shabby old vintage T-bird redone with great care. I looked over at my wife, who stood there with a smirk on her face.

"It's about time," she said. "Roselita's niece called before we left and asked me what the car needed. I, of course, said everything. She asked me what colors you liked and I picked these out. I remembered you admiring one like it. So I gave her the key while we were away. What do you think?"

"It's amazing." Now I was not known as a car buff; just something to get me from one place to another. "Now, I have a showpiece."

"Not only that, Roselita's friend replaced all kinds of things on the engine, and places I don't even know about. He said it would be like brand new."

"It certainly looks it. I guess this is my fee. I certainly did well by her, and I've been taken care of."

I f loated into my den in the house which was now my office and checked my phone messages.

Lt. Mehle had checked in to say the two cops, both the one from Philly and the AG agent who gotten their union reps to intercede and were deciding what to do. No offers had been made. Similarly, Sgt. McCready checked in to say Peter Lynch had lawyered up and would be of no help.

I wondered if the DA had enough to go after anyone. Based on Carmen's testimony, they had proof of a prostitution ring and a drug dealing operation at the bar against its owner—whoever he was. They had Peter Lynch possibly complicit in the prostitution. The Liquor Control Board might yank the bar's license for some period of time. Given Carmen's ID of the decedent as the delivery man of the drugs to the bar, it was not entirely clear that his murder could be linked to the bar. Because Carmen was a cooperating witness who had made a deal with the DA, her testimony alone might not be strong enough to support any drug claim against the bar by the Liquor Control Board. I had done well by my client, but the bad guys were still unscathed.

My next messages came from Roselita's daughter whose English was pure American. "Mr. Magen. A number of men have been calling here asking where Carmen is."

I called Roselita's daughter back. "Did these men ask for Carmen or Flora?"

"No. They asked for Carmen. Who is Flora?"

"Well, that's another story. So just Carmen. Were they Hispanic or what?"

"Definitely Hispanic, but not Honduran. Probably Mexican." "Great. Thanks." I hung up and began to think.

Uh oh. Someone's cage had been rattled. The question was: whose cage and by whom?

Only a few people knew about Carmens cooperation—Lt. Mehle and Sgt. McCready and the DA's office. These people are usually very careful about releasing information about who is cooperating; but someone might have put two and two together to figure who might be a witness against them. Whoever that was was getting the jitters and was risking a play against Carmen. They had done their homework and knew that Flora was

Carmen. Roselita had been given a cell number to contact Carmen, but, as a usual precaution, she did not know her actual location and the cell phone number was posted through a remote location and was hooked up to trace all calls to that number. I felt Carmen herself was safe, but I called her anyway to alert her to any possibilities.

CHAPTER TWENTY-EIGHT

Golf Course Attack

It was a bright spring day for the team tournament of the golf club. Threesomes and foursomes dressed in outlandish colors rarely found any place in nature except on the golf course on which white middle aged men were putting and awaiting their tee-off times. Trash talking was abundant as the respective team members attempted to interfere with the concentration of their opponents. After all, as much as $50 each rode on the outcome of today's match but the prize of gloating in the bar afterward was priceless.

My foursome consisted of two low handicap players and the club rule maven. He was punctilious in the enforcement of all of golf's many and often arcane rules, and even made up a few just if no one was paying attention. It was early in the season and my swing had not approached the mid summer fluidity it required; but my score was an essential element in the team scoring. The team captain teed off early and drove around the golf course checking on each team member's progress. He had lost the team title the previous year by a few strokes after leading the entire tournament and was not a bit happy about it. He had been royally roasted by the club's number one jester at the draft this year and behind a stiff smile smoke could be seen emanating from his ears and nostrils.

This was pressure. Golf requires a series of even relaxed repetitive swings, yet with its rules, its betting, its team events, it puts constant pressure on the mind. As Yogi Berra says, "ninety percent of this game is half mental." I with my bogeyful handicap did not need this pressure, but somehow sought it out. Was this fun?

Sports has an unusual way of separating out people. The good athletes when kids are young play the most popular sports—baseball, football, basketball and learn those skills early. By the time they reach their twenties they can't play those sports anymore except in a few old men's leagues. People outgrow other sports as well—wrestling, gymnastics, hockey. But golf and tennis go on forever; but there is a reversal. The kids who learned those sports very early in life are the best in those sports in later life and can look down on the good athletes from their early years who are left with nothing but memories of glory days.

So our time to tee off started. I could still hit the ball long with the better golfers, but, when it came to touch and technique, I was lost. As a result, when my ball landed in one of my familiar landing areas, the hazard on the fifth hole, I had to climb through bushes to get to it with my 7 iron in hand to pull it out from the foliage.

Of course, I could not find it, but came away with two callaways and a srixon which kept my financial loss in check. As I came thrashing out of the bushes, hacking away with my 7 iron, I saw two of the grounds crew waiting for me. And then, the light broke through. It wasn't the grounds crew; one of the men was Emilio the bartender from Tito's looking at me with great interest. Behind him was a van with its motor running and next to him was another burly fellow. I could see him reaching inside his coveralls. He was after me, and he wanted to know where Carmen was. He wouldn't kill me, but he would want to kidnap me.

As the two men approached, some animal instinct took over, and I gripped the 7 iron in two hands and swung at the bartender's hand that was beginning to emerge from his coveralls. The head of the iron hit him squarely on the wrist—those days on the practice range were paying off. He yelped and dropped the gun. I swung at the other husky guy and hit him in the nether region where his privates hung, giving his reproductive gear a sturdy clout. He fell to the ground, groaning in miserable gasps. The bartender lunged at me, but with only one good hand, before I buried the head of the iron in the back of his skull as he ran past.

The entire melee had attracted my playing partners who came running over to see what was going on. By this time, I was bent over with my hands on my knees, vomiting a very nice breakfast. My knees were shaking so badly I was having trouble standing. I managed to croak out, "Call 911 and get the gun." The bartender was out cold, but the other man was in a fetal crouch holding his injured member. Neither attacker presented much of a threat.

The police were on the scene in due time and took me to the side to lean against a berm. I must have been coherent to them because they took the two men into custody with the paddy wagon which showed up later. They took me to the clubhouse. After a few gulps of water, I was able to tell them the whole story and had them contact Sgt. McCready and Lt. Mehle. They showed me the gun which turned out to be a taser. My shaking had subsided and I could stand without my knees wobbling.

Slowly, the threesomes and foursomes from the tournament began to come in from the their rounds. Of course, the rumor of the events of my attack had circulated around the course. A large conglomeration of members were now in the bar area asking for details. My own foursome ably and with a good deal of exaggeration described the exploits they had been able to observe. They even produced my 7 iron wrapped in a hand towel.

One of the first comments came from one of the better pundits grinning over his beer mug. "Why a 7 iron, Dave? Were you going for distance or trajectory?"

Another chimed in. "No. It's the weapon of choice. If it was good enough for Tiger's wife, it's good enough for everyone."

Another wit: "Did you clear your hips on the swing, or did you use an open stance?"

Another: "Which ball did you get, the left or the right?"

One of the lawyers in the group said that the wife of the man who suffered the injured reproductive equipment would be suing me for loss of consortium. Another suggested that his right hand would be suing for loss of consortium.

Another: "Don't ask Magen for any strokes. Especially with a 7 iron in his hand."

As I tried to chortle lamely, the crew grew rowdier.

Another: "I saw the guy's head. Does this count as a hole in one? If so, Dave's buying." For non golfers, a hole in one on the course that day, obligates the player to pay for drinks for the day.

Eventually, the member of my foursome that was the rule maven spoke up. "Well fellas. I hate to say this but I'd have to give him a two stroke penalty for grounding his club in the hazard and make him replay the shot from where he took the first swing. He also has to count each of the three swings." The team captain furiously argued the ruling and wanted to know if I could finish the round now, which sparked a furious debate with the rules committee. Another group started to discuss the design of a plaque to commemorate this event in club history and mark it on the spot of the fight. Eventually, they began to look at the 7 iron and saw that in the last swing I had broken the hozzle (the piece that holds the blade to the club shaft.) The pro said the club had to be forfeited to be placed over the bar, but he would order me a replacement.

One of the women wanted to know why they hadn't been equally attacked on the course. The lady's husband commented that he was too tired, but he was okay with it if someone wanted to step in.

My shaking had almost subsided and my lame smile was now stuck on my face.

CHAPTER TWENTY-NINE

Mehle and Me Meet After Golf Course Incident

L t. Mehle had wanted to go over the events at the golf course and made an appointment to meet me with Sgt. McCready at my house. They pulled up in my driveway just as I was finishing my breakfast; soft-boiled eggs, English muffin and green tea. As they came in, they both nodded. "Nice house," McCready said. We lived in a nice old neighborhood of West Mount Airy which was filled with houses built over one hundred years ago. It was no longer a wealthy neighborhood but housed many of the judges, doctors, lawyers and professors who worked in Philadelphia. It was also a very integrated community with many mixed racial marriages and many gay and lesbian couples. This was not the usual turf for either policeman.

"Can I get you some tea?" I offered. These two younger men were obviously not into healthy practices and declined. "Please have a seat and let me know what has happened."

The two men drew up chairs to the breakfast table and opened their notebooks.

McCready began. "Well, your friend the bartender awoke after twenty-four hours and had a very large lump on his cocoa. I think the other fellow is still crouched in a fetal position holding his 'huevos.' You did a serious number on them."

"The adrenal glands were in high gear. I still don't know how I managed it. But why me? Why would they think of an attack on me?"

A slight change in tone from McCready. "They think you were blackmailing them or might interfere with some deal they had made." With that both cops stopped and looked at me for a reaction. Was I? "Me? Blackmail? No way. My work on the case was done. My client was out of danger and had no charges. I felt my job was done.

What did he say?"

"He says you were squeezing his partner in the bar. He claims he was going to own half the bar and that you were going to kill the deal. His one chance at big money."

"Who was his partner? Did he say?" "Not yet."

"I have some ideas. See the title to the bar is in the name of a secretary of the Lynch law firm. They do a ton of liquor work. The secretary was put in as the owner of the bar supposedly because some drug dealer who had a felony conviction could not get a license from the Liquor Control Board so Peter Lynch put the title in his secretary's name and was charging him a monthly fee for this privilege. So Peter Lynch controls title to the bar.

"My guess was that the drug dealer who was killed in the black Escalade was the owner. With him dead, no one except Lynch could claim title to the bar. So he made a deal with the bartender to run it for him and keep some percentage of the drug proceeds. That's my guess. It makes sense. Especially since Carmen identified the dead drug dealer as the one who brought the bartender the beer boxes with the coke packages.

"The drug dealer must have found the source of the coke and made his own deal."

The two detectives were writing away on their pads furiously as I spoke.

They went over my dates and names and my theory for about a half hour.

Asking the same questions in different ways.

Finally, Mehle spoke. He was to be the good cop—the guy I knew. "Mr. Magen, what did you get for handling this case?"

I knew this was confidential client information and I could well have told him so. In fact, I did; but then I told him it was of little consequence so I told him anyway. "Carmen has of course paid me nothing. Sometime after the first court appearances, a guy in a purple mustang with Jersey plates came to my house and dropped off $2000 in bills." Something told me not to tell him about the fact that I kept the bills untouched in my freezer. "I never heard from him again. I don't know who gave him the money or why. I don't even know why I was given the money. I assumed someone wanted to help Carmen so that she would not cooperate and give up her boss. If she plead guilty as a minor, she would only get a slap on the wrist and no criminal penalty. "The only other thing was someone fixed up my car. After the charges against Carmen were dropped and she got immunity, we went away on vacation for a week. While I was gone, someone got the car keys from my wife and took the car. When it came back, my somewhat elegantly shabby 2002 black Thunderbird had a dark metallic red custom paint job and brand new maroon upholstery. I am now the envy of all my golf buddies. Some friend of Carmen's did it."

"That's all?"

"That's it."

"Did she convey any…ahem…favors on you?"

Now, I was getting a little pissed. This was not proper, and it was a confidential communication they were asking about. "Now. Stop right there. That's a serious accusation. Why are you doing this?"

"We need to clear you completely."

"Then. No. I'm a retired lawyer with forty-six years experience in the legal system. She's a minor and client. Wrong on both counts. You got that? Wrong." I was pissed.

The cops looked at each other and waited for me to calm down. "Did you buy her anything?"

"Wait. I'm the lawyer. She's the client. She's supposed to pay me." "We get that, but, Mr. Magen, it's important to ask. Please trust me."

"Okay, I bought her breakfast twice. Both at the Aramingo Diner. The first after she spent the night in jail after her arrest and the second after her hearing. I also bought her lunch once at an AW stand. That's it. "It gave me the opportunity to conduct a full interview and get the facts together."

"Other than that, were you ever alone together?"

"No, except while I drove her in my car from court to the diner, or from the diner to her aunt's place.

"What's this about?"

"Well, accusations have been made. We need to clear them up before we can let you in on what's happening."

"Okay. So, no—I did not have sex with that woman. (Unlike Bill Clinton.) No—I got no other money. No—I did not blackmail anyone—I have no interest in a flea-bitten drug bar. Yes—he attacked me, and I acted in self-defense on my own golf course. What else do you want to know?"

"Mr. Magen. If we believed any of this, we would have read you your rights. We didn't. You know that. We can't use your statement against you. But we have a lot of things to go over with you and needed to clear you. Your reputation precedes you. Now, here's what we have so far.

"The bartender is still in the hospital, but is under arrest for aggravated assault and attempted kidnapping. They had chloroform and ropes in the van along with plastic hand and leg restraints. I assume they were going to take you somewhere. They other guy was just muscle along for the ride. He doesn't know anything.

"As far as the two cops, we sweated the Philadelphia cop. He claims he doesn't know the other cop and did this on his own. We have the CDs from the bar and it shows two undercover cops. The AG's office has no record of any AG officer being involved."

"Okay. I have an idea there. Peter Lynch was well connected with the Liquor Control Board and their enforcement division. They recently came under the jurisdiction of the State Police, but not under the AG's office. He could have been working for the LCB and called himself an AG agent. In that way, Peter Lynch would have had access to him."

"I see. Well. We'll check that out."

"What about Lynch? He's the most logical to be the bartender's partner.

When I first started my investigation, I was approached by Liam Lynch— Peter's father. He offered me some money not to have Carmen implicate his firm in any plea deal. I rejected the idea because I did not think I should compromise any of her options. Later, Peter Lynch called me up and complained that I was blackmailing him. I was not but he may have believed I was."

"What about the forensics on the shooting of the drug dealer owner?"

"He is Juan Diaz, a Dominican with a criminal record for drugs. He was on the DEA radar screen and had made a few sales to undercover agents, but had not yet been arrested."

"So if he had been arrested, he might not have been killed. He was probably killed for ownership of the bar."

"Seems so."

"But did the bartender kill him?"

"We can't tell if it may have been a contract hit."

"I think that the most important thing would be to identify the source of the cocaine supply; but without the bartender I don't know who will own the place."

"At this point, we will re-interview Peter Lynch and then we may want to re-interview Carmen about who hung out at the bar."

As the two cops walked out of the house, they both detoured over to look at my Thunderbird. "Nice ride," they both murmured.

CHAPTER THIRTY

Liam Lynch Calls

I was surfing casually in front of my computer screen (that's what you do when you're retired) when the phone jangled on my old office line. "Mr. Magen, Liam Lynch here, can we talk?"

It was Liam Lynch out of the blue. What could he want? I was sure his son was in on this murder business, and since Carmen and I were out, I thought it was over. "Yes, Liam. What can I do for you?" Liam was always an old school gentlemen and hard to say no to.

"My son and I would like to meet downtown for lunch when you're available."

Being semi-retired means you're almost always available. "Sure, Liam. You name the time."

"The sooner the better. How about at 1:30 today?" I could already taste the great food at his club. "Fine. See you then."

It was a warm day as I parked and walked to the club. Liam and Peter were already seated as I was directed to the table. I had been thinking about Crab Imperial the whole way down and was not about to deny myself. They ordered. They were both beefy Irishmen with rounded faces and ordered cherrystones to start, and tilapias to follow. Beers materialized in front of them. I knew if I had a beer today I wouldn't be able to remember where I left the car.

"So, Liam. Always a pleasure to dine with you. What can I do?"

Peter spoke first, he was nervous and looked shamefaced. "It's me, Mr. Magen. I might need your help. I think you know most of what's going on and we feel we can trust you."

109

"Aha." I could feel a large ideogram passing in front of my eyes—watch out! I knew immediately I had a conflict of interest with Carmen that might have already been resolved. I knew Liam was a decent and respected guy, but this Peter was a loose cannon. He could cause me some serious pain, but the Crab Imperial was really good so I had to hear him out. "You know first, I might have a conflict of interest—I have represented the little prostitute in the bar. I guess you know I was attacked by the bartender."

"We heard that. I swear I had nothing to do with that. That's why I'm here."

"Alright. I'll listen, but back at your office where we can have some privacy."

"Fair enough." We agreed to meet at the Lynch firm at 3PM.

When we reassembled, I'd had enough time to collect my thoughts and raise several hundred deal breaker questions. I was ushered into a stylish old conference room with a big mahogany table and about twenty chairs. On the walls were some old oil paintings of Irish countrysides, churches, and farmsteads. Liam and I sat at the head of the table. He was still wearing a tweed suit with a vest that actually had lapels. Peter was sitting to his father's right, he had his suit jacket on the back of the chair and had already undone his tie.

I sat opposite Peter. "Okay, first question: why me?"

Peter glanced nervously at his father. "I can't trust any of the regular criminal attorneys. They have too many connections with too many bad guys and I think they might sell me out. I know you do some criminal work, but I also know it's mostly court-appointed now and you've never been in with the criminal bar."

"That's true." I was an independent. For the most part, the everyday criminal bar all knew each other. They often referred cases among themselves and cooperated in their defenses. Their clients rarely ratted each other out except by special understanding. I handled mostly what are known as white collar criminal cases. These were usually first time offenders who were involved in complicated business deals that most criminal defense lawyers didn't understand. For that matter, the criminal prosecutors mostly never understood the deals and required special help from experts from the Treasury or the FBI to be able to explain it to a jury.

"I never meant to get into this and I'm in over my head. I need someone who can make a practical business deal and get me out of this entire mess. I need a kind of maverick business lawyer who can talk to some bad guys."

"Uh-huh. So you're not looking for a defense to a crime. You're trying to make a deal."

"Exactly."

"First, I have to have the truth from you. From the beginning and leaving nothing out. Otherwise, I could get caught up in this thing as one of your accomplices. I won't be put in the middle." I could see Liam slowly writing out a check and I could feel myself slowly getting sucked in.

"Second. I do the talking. No negotiating behind my back. I am the sole mouthpiece."

"Fine. As long as we agree where you're going with this." "Of course. No problem."

"I may have to keep the police in the loop as things develop. If you want to get out of this yourself, you're going to have to show good faith and supply them with information. Otherwise, it could backfire and they could go after you."

"Understood."

"Okay. Tell me the story. Has your father heard it yet?"

"Yes he has. And I want him to hear it again. I've made a mistake and I don't want to blow it again."

"Okay, what's happened?"

"As you know, it started out innocently enough. Well not innocently. I had a client who was a drug dealer with a felony conviction who wanted to buy a bar. I explained he couldn't get a liquor license with a felony record, so I agreed to get him a phony owner for a fee. My secretary could use a few extra bucks and so could I so we rented him the license for $1000 per month. I didn't realize he would put girls and drugs in there, but as it developed it wasn't so bad. I got a spot where I could entertain a few friends for free and the place ran pretty well. I didn't realize it was making so much money.

"The place began to attract some envy. Someone figured out that I was the owner and wanted to buy it from me. As they explained 'I wasn't cut out to deal.' That much was true but I made the mistake of asking how we would get rid of the real owner. He said leave it to me."

"Who was this?"

"He gave me a card that said he was a lawyer from Trenton. A Hispanic guy. As I later discovered, he was a phony, acting for someone else.

"I explained I couldn't sell it, because I didn't own it. The next thing I knew, these cops came in and raided the place for vice, not drugs, but vice. I thought that was weird, and then the guy called me up and asked if I was ready to sell. I explained again that I didn't own it. "I knew something was very screwy. I didn't get arrested, nor did the girl I was with. They let the judge go and just arrested Flora. They never searched the place. They never questioned the bartender. That was it. It was a warning to me to sell the bar. The next phone call, I must have made the mistake of giving out the real owner's name. That was the last I heard from anyone and the next thing I knew the owner was dead, and the cops suspected me."

"First things first: did you know Flora?" "Except for that night, never."

"Do you use drugs?"

"Except for some grass now and then, no." "No coke?"

"No coke!"

"There was some in the judge's and Flora's room. Did you know about that?"

"No. No idea."

"Did you know the woman you were with?" "No. Before that night. No."

"How about the bartender?"

"Of course I said hello when I came in and got the key. I knew his name."

"Did you know he was selling drugs out of the bar?" "Yes. I guess I did."

"The only benefit you got from the sale of drugs was the monthly payment to serve as show owner?"

"That was it."

"No other benefits?"

"None. Other than an occasional free ride for one of my friends."

"How many times did you do that?"

"About nine."

"I'll need a list of who they were. Anyone prominent like the judge?"

"There were three lawyers, four clients, and two bankers who lent my clients money to buy bars." "I'll need a list."

"You got it. I'm writing now as we speak."

"I'm just thinking off the top of my head here, but just what do you expect me to do? I think we can simply lay our cards on the table with the police and, from what you're telling me, you will not be held for any criminal charges, if we cooperate. Of course, you may have done a few things that the Liquor Control Board doesn't like, but that's just an administrative penalty. You may get a fine or a suspension but your relationship with the LCB over the years will certainly help you there. You know what that all means better than I do. So, at a minimum, I could weave you through the criminal system without you being charged.

"The other possibility is this. You are the owner of a valuable asset, on paper at least. There is no paperwork to connect your ownership of the bar, the real estate, the liquor license at all to the dead man who was your client and I don't see anyone stepping forward to claim his interest. Someone wants that bar, and you have the ability at least to shut it down. It is a valuable retail location—let's call it that. If it's shut down even for a little while, it loses its value as an attraction for druggies. You certainly don't want to be in the business of running a retail drug operation. Do you?"

"Of course not."

"Someone is running it now. The real owner is dead, the bartender who operated is in custody."

"Thanks to you."

"Yes. Thank you very much for that. I think my heart rate is still not back to normal. Okay. Now somebody has to deliver drugs to the bar, someone has to pick up the proceeds and someone has to sell the drugs. Now, if that's not you and it's not the bartender, it has to be someone. I suspect whoever is doing it is the one who killed the former owner, and may have instigated the raid by the cops."

"So what do we do?"

"As we speak the cops are probably conducting a surveillance on the bar, and may have even done a few buys. They know it is a drug location and they're going to want to make some arrests, and then find out who killed the owner. You're looking at a dangerous situation here. My safest advice is to come clean with the cops, make a deal for immunity and get yourself cleaned up with the LCB. The cops, if they make some drug arrests there, will forfeit the bar, the real estate and the liquor license and sell it all off. You'll get nothing but you'll be clean. That is my most conservative advice."

"What if someone wants to buy it from me? Can I sell it to him?"

"Hmm. First, you know it is a 'dirty' location. The liquor license could be in jeopardy and so could the real estate. You can't give any warranties that it is clean."

"But what if they still want to buy it?"

My sense was definitely alert now. Someone had already approached him and he wanted to see what he could make on the deal and how much trouble he could get into. "Aha! So we have a buyer. How did this happen?"

"Someone approached me even before the raid. They wanted to know if it was for sale. I explained that I was not the real owner and that he would have to talk to the real owner."

"Did you tell him the real owner's name?"

"No. I didn't want this guy to have some thing on me what with the title being in Margret Mary's name. So I said I would speak to the real owner."

"What happened next?"

"The bar was raided by the cops with me in it."

"Aha! Did you put two and two together and figure out that you were being given a warning?"

"Not at first. I asked the owner, and the bartender. I was pissed because I was somehow in the middle and I'd gotten the judge in trouble, but they knew nothing about it. I asked them about the guy who wanted to buy the place and they brushed it off as a nuisance."

"What did he look like?"

"He was a small white man with a pencil mustache who drove up in a purple mustang with a white stripe and Jersey plates."

"That's interesting. A loose end. That's the same man who came up to me and gave me $2000 for Flora's defense. I wonder how he's connected? In any case, what do you want me to do? Get you out clean with the cops and abandon the bar, or try to sell the bar and then settle with the cops?"

Peter looked at his father who was deep in thought staring out the window.

Eventually, Liam looked back at us.

"Gentlemen. We have no connection with the drug trade, nor do we want any. We don't own this bar, the liquor license or the real estate, but, at this point, no one else does either. We can't deliver good title, or warrant the transfer of the liquor license.

"It would be dishonorable to represent that we can. However, we can deliver a 'quit claim deed' and a 'power of attorney' to whoever wants to control the bar. That's not dishonest. It terminates in a clean way an interest and has a great value to the new owner whoever he is. We don't know anything, we don't represent anything, we don't sell anything, but if someone wants to pay for whatever we have we'll sell it to them. Mr. Magen, see if you can approach these people with that proposition and negotiate a price. You'll get a 25% commission against your retainer for your efforts. I'll prepare all the necessary paperwork. Do you think you can do this?"

I ran through all the possibilities in my head. I couldn't think of anything criminal that we would be doing. If I properly represented what we knew about the problems the bar was facing with the police and a possible forfeiture, and left the solution to those problems up to the buyer, I wouldn't be doing anything fraudulent. They were assuming the risk with full disclosure of the facts. It sounded plausible. I wouldn't have a conflict with Carmen, she was safe and out of the way and wouldn't be involved in the future. Yes. It seemed doable.

Liam was already sliding the $10,000 check for my retainer across the table.

"Mr. Magen, see what you can do." This was going to be interesting.

CHAPTER THIRTY-ONE

Magen Revisits Bar

With a fresh $10,000 retainer check in my back pocket, I went first to the bank and then home to change into my latino working man's outfit for a visit to the bar; dusty khakis, a rumpled pullover and a large cross on my chest hair. The afternoon crowd was filtering in. I brought along a Gameboy—a great surveillance tool. It would let me sit for long periods of time, permit me to avoid conversation with anyone nearby and allow me plenty of time to observe the comings and goings. To my delight, the bar still carried Rolling Rock and I happily sat down at a wonderful angle to observe the bar and sip the formerly popular suds from my youth.

The bartender was new, of course. The customers did not seem to know him and he volunteered little conversation. They got their beers and sat down. The hot dogs on the roller had not changed since my last visit. A few more turns and they might be ready for the Smithsonian as archaeological relics. Or maybe, they could be used to cut industrial diamonds.

I couldn't see anything that looked like drug traffic: no furtive glances by the customers, no in and out customers who did not buy an adult beverage, and no reaching under the bar for small packages. By the same token, I did not see anything that looked like an undercover narc—the customers were latino, most were speaking Spanish; of course, it might be difficult to pick up a good narc.

Finally, a few drug buys seemed to take place. Customers with a few large bills got little or no change, left with a small baggy slid carefully along the bar out of plain view, and then a departure without a drink. Some of the buys were larger in size; possibly eight balls— enough to break down or resell after cooking as crack. So we might have a mini-wholesale operation going as well. I could not hear the transaction to tell whether there was some password or call sign to vouch for the buyer's bona fide. But there was definitely some traffic. After enough time to satisfy my curiosity, I decided I would approach the bartender. He was a surly guy, and not pleasant. I made a note not to hire him for the neighborhood tavern. I did my best latino accent.

"So, mang. Can I get a bag?"

"No way, I don't do that." Apparently, I needed a call sign even for a bag— an eight ball was out of the question. So I stood up a little straighter and sounding in my best authoritative lawyer tones, and reaching in my wallet for my card. I said, "Tell your boss to contact me. I represent the owner if he wants to buy." The bartender scowled an even darker scowl, but he took the card. I backed away from the bar to avoid any possible baseball bat the bartender had under the counter, I waved at the camera located to my right, and left the scene. Before I got in my car, I walked up and down the block to see if I could spot some police surveillance. There didn't appear to be any. No vans, no men dozing in their cars, no large antennas.

I was getting the idea that the police were not interested.

Carmen took the bus home to New Jersey from her boarding school to live with her uncle's family while still as a protected witness. We notified the police who alerted the local New Jersey police in Vineland.

She gave me a call to let me know how things had gone at school. She had been released on bail into my custody, so I was still responsible for her.

"So Mr. Stern, I'm back after the summer. They want me back for the full year. I can graduate next year. I made up my classes from Father Judge."

"That's great, Carmen. So what was school like?"

"At first, the girls were a little snooty, so I stuck to myself and studied. They are very strict here and you have to remain in your room like a convent. So I caught up on my math and English."

"Wonderful."

"Well, not so. They had a sex ed class taught by this older lady."

"So sex ed in Catholic school?"

"Yeah, you got that. This lady hadn't been properly shtupped, so at night I had to fill some of the girls in. That made me real popular. I mean they had some of the weirdest fantasies and dreams. Pretty soon, I was real popular. I mean this school should give me a professorship. It seems like they think sex ed is just 'grin and bear it.'"

"I'm happy to hear you're able to help." I was wondering what it would be like for all these Irish and Italian boys they'd be dating.

"And they had these religion classes. I mean we had a few at Father Judge, but just the basic Jesus stuff. Here, we got St. Augustine and Thomas Aquinas. And then, there was the lady our school was named after, St. Teresa of Avila. Definitely a weird one. What is it with Catholic women and sex.

"But it's a nice place and I got good grades. I'll be in some of the smart kids classes this fall."

"That's great. I knew you could do it.

CHAPTER THIRTY-TWO

Brushoff from McCready

Lt. Mehle was a good cop and I was pleased to have a decent relationship with him. McCready was a different matter. After Mehle basically lost jurisdiction in the case, I would have to deal with McCready. After all, the cop Mehle would have been interested in had made an arrest—a cheesy little one, but an arrest. The cop had covered up a judge and the other prostitute and Peter Lynch as well as drug dealings at the bar. But a murder was a murder and that was McCready's bailiwick.

When I called McCready, I knew in the very tone of his voice, I was getting no cooperation and McCready had little interest in the bar. I was bothering him and he let me know it.

"Detective, David Magen here. I just wanted to follow up…" "Okay sure. Nothing to tell yet."

"I went out to the bar to see who was running it…" "What did you do that for?"

"With the owner dead, I needed to see who was running the place and whether they were still dealing…"

"Dealing what?" I knew he knew I meant dealing drugs, but he didn't like a lawyer using cop slang. He was letting me know he was the professional allowed to use cop slang and I was a nuisance.

"Drugs. Isn't that what this is about?" I refrained from adding 'you ignorant asshole,' but that was implied.

"Oh yeah. Well this is a homicide and we're still doing crime scene."

"Doesn't seem likely that the one who took over the drug trade after the murder is the one who committed the murder. If there was some surveillance on the bar wouldn't that lead you to the new owner?" "Yeah. Good idea, counselor. I'll think about that." Anytime a cop calls me counselor, I know he is telling me all lawyers are nuisances, all cops are way too street smart to actually listen to a lawyer. "I had some information on the new owner…"

"Fine. I'll give you a call when I need it."

This was going nowhere. He wasn't going to cooperate with me and I was now released from any obligation to cooperate with him. I could make my deal in peace and he could go to hell, the arrogant prick.

CHAPTER THIRTY-THREE

Magen Visits Mehle

I had a sneaking feeling that the bar issues had been put on the back burner by the police. On the one hand, it would make my deal with the latest drug dealer easier, but it made me feel as a citizen that I was not getting my money's worth from the local constabulary. So I called Mehle—I could always get the straight scoop from him.

"Lieutenant, Magen here! I'm still involved with this business of Tito's bar. I went down to take a look at it yesterday and it looks like there's no police activity. The bar is up and running with a new bartender."

"Mr. Magen. Oh yes. The bar. Well, as you know I'm IAD, not homicide. While you and I think some cops may have pulled off the raid and not filed a full report, there's nothing to back this up. So far, the cop involved did arrest a juvenile prostitute, but she was let go along with the john. That doesn't give me much to go on. And the murder of the alleged owner—that's in homicide's lap so I backed off. That's department policy."

"But the bar. We know that's a drug sale location." "Yes. But then, that's not my jurisdiction either."

"They may be doing something, maybe not. I wouldn't know." "Hmm. Okay. Well, that's for the update."

CHAPTER THIRTY-FOUR

Purple Mustang Returns

As I returned from the gym the next day, I was feeling relaxed and happy. The gym always did that. I was tired, but my mind was active and positive. I felt creative and energetic. And there in my driveway was the purple Mustang with the Jersey plates. I was sure to write the plate number down this time. As the driver, who was sitting in the front seat saw me, he signaled to let him out so I could pull in. After our cars were reversed, he got out of the car and came up to me. He was the same slight figure. "Can we talk?" he said.

I was sure that he was responding to the business card I left at the bar just two days ago. This quick response was a good sign—I had a willing buyer. "Sure, come on in."

We came in and sat at the breakfast table. I went to the refrigerator and asked him if he wanted a soda. When he accepted, I was even more sure that I had a buyer. I opened my sandwich and sat opposite him. "What can I do for you?"

"You left your card at Tito's and said your client wanted to sell. We're interested."

"Good. But I have to tell you a few things up front. I don't want you to be disappointed.

"First, my client doesn't really own it. I believe the drug dealer who died, Juan Diaz, was the real owner and that my client was acting as the straw owner for him since he could not hold a liquor license because of a prior felony conviction."

"We know that."

"Good. So my client will only give you a 'quit claim' deed. Since we don't own it, we can't give you good title. You just get what we have, which may be nothing."

"We know that."

"I can't promise you anything except that we won't interfere with you operating the bar. You will have a management agreement that lets you operate the bar until the liquor license is transferred to you."

"We know that."

The guy was a lot more savvy than he looked. "I have to say that I was attacked personally by Emilio, the prior bartender. He must have thought I controlled something and he wanted to threaten or control me somehow. I am just the lawyer, I don't own anything and I do what my client tells me."

"We know that. We had nothing to do with the attack and we have no interest in harming you or your client."

"Okay. So far so good. Now I will deliver a quit claim deed to the real estate, a management agreement so that you can operate the bar, and a sales agreement for the bar business and the liquor license. You will have to handle all arrangements to transfer the liquor license yourself. We will not guarantee we own it or that the license can even be transferred."

"We know that."

"Very good. This deal must be all cash upfront."

"We know that." He wasn't very original but this was getting easier than I thought.

"The previous sale for the real estate, the business and the liquor license was for $200,000."

"We know that." Very interesting. Somehow he had become aware of the prior transactions. The public records only showed a sale of $100,000.

"This business may be involved in criminal activities, and may make a considerable amount of money doing so."

"We know that." This was the right guy I was talking to.

"The business as it now operates may require a dependable source of illegal items in the future."

"We know that."

"If someone from the prior owner should come forward and have evidence of his ownership, his estate may contest your ownership and you could lose everything."

"We'll take that risk." I'll bet they would. "Okay. What's your offer?"

"Since you can't give us a good title, but we can operate the bar without your claim to it, we can't offer the $200,000. A liquor license is worth $75,000 and the real estate may be worth $100,000. The business value is unknown. We offer $150,000 cash, settlement within fifteen days, we prepare the paperwork. We need releases and quit claims from both Lynches and you."

"I will convey this to my client and get back to you. Who are you and how can I reach you?"

"My name is Roy Dwyer and my cell phone number is 609-555- 1212." A Jersey number. No address. Could this be his real name?

"Fine, I'll call you as soon as I know something."

CHAPTER THIRTY-FIVE

Telephone Call to Mehle After Purple Mustang

I knew I was tiptoeing on the edge of the law with this deal with Roy Dwyer. After all, my client and I knew the bar was a drug sales location. Although we had nothing to do with starting it up or operating it now, someone was operating it as such and would continue to do so. By ridding ourselves of any involvement in it for a price, we were somehow making money from the deal. We also knew that a deceased drug dealer actually owned the bar, and we were in effect selling his interest. However, the deceased drug dealer had been engaged in an illegal activity which we had neither condoned nor participated in. Since no one was likely to come in and claim his interest, because they would have to admit some knowledge of the illegal activity in doing so. And now, here is the beauty part. My client had instructed me to do so and he had full knowledge of the events. I had also made a complete disclosure to the buyer.

Technically, Peter Lynch and his secretary had breached what we call a fiduciary duty to the deceased drug dealer by profiting from the sale of the bar. But as a fiduciary, Lynch owed a duty of loyalty to the deceased drug dealer. However, when Lynch discovered his activity as a show pony for the drug dealer involved him in criminal activity, he had a right to purge himself of his illegality. If he sold out the drug dealer's interest he had a duty to hold the proceeds for the drug dealer or his heir. Of course, these proceeds could be forfeited. I so advised Lynch in a letter to cover my butt, but he shrugged and said he would put the money in his escrow account for four years—the applicable period for the statute of limitations.

After I analyzed all that, I was feeling a bit cleaner. Morally, of course, I should admit that I knew I was aiding the Lynches to use their position as trusted agents of the deceased drug dealer to sell off the illegal assets of their client. On the other hand, these assets were severely limited because their client used them in a criminal enterprise. However, these assets were being sold to someone who would continue to use them in the same criminal enterprise. However, he would use them in the same criminal enterprise with or without a sale. It was clearly a mixed bag of moral judgments as well as legal entanglements.

In any case, the bar once the drug activity was discovered by the police would be forfeited in any case and sold off. The liquor license would be moved to a new location, and the real estate would be put to some legal retail use. So the moral and legal scales would end balanced.

To that end, I thought I should stay in touch with Lt. Mehle. McCready was a pigheaded jerk who was not interested in my input and I certainly was not going to let him gain credit for any arrests or forfeitures. But Lt. Mehle deserved my help. So I called him. It certainly would mark me as a good guy on the moral scale by hastening the end of the drug traffic and solving the murder. By letting him in on the information would certainly deflect any criminal investigator from me and my clients.

"Lt. Mehle, David Magen here."

"Ah, Mr. Magen. What can I do for you?"

"I wanted to give you some information. McCready has rejected any of my help, but I wanted to put a few ideas in your head."

"Always happy to have your input. What's up?"

"As you know the Lynch's secretary is the nominal holder of the real estate and the liquor license. Someone has been operating the bar—probably as a drug sale operation since the death of the prior owner. We don't know who this is. It's just a bartender, but he's not ours and we don't know who he works for. So I offered to sell the bar to his boss—whoever he is. And I got a response; but I know this is not the real buyer. I wanted to run my information by you."

"Okay. What have you got?"

"The man introduced himself as 'Roy Dwyer' and he drove a purple mustang with New Jersey plates CPJ-5354 and he gave me his telephone cell number as 609-555-1212. That's all I have so far."

"I'll check it out."

"I'd appreciate it if you could give me the results. I'm a little afraid I am walking into a trap. I've already been attacked once and Ms. Magen doesn't want to lose her source of income."

"Sure, Mr. Magen. I'll let you know."

CHAPTER THIRTY-SIX

Telephone Calls to Lynches and Mehle and Leslie

The next call was to the very joyous Lynches that they had a deal and could "sell" something they didn't own. I would call Dwyer and tell him to proceed with the paperwork.

Lt. Mehle also called me back the next day. "Mr. Magen, not great news. First, Roy Dwyer does not exist in PA or NJ or on the NCIC list of convicted persons. His cell number is a burn phone which has been traced to a number of locations in New Jersey—mostly large commercial areas, no residences. His license plate is out of service in New Jersey and it was previously in a corporate name by a large public company on an older Chevy Malibu. This guy is a very cagey customer. Watch out. He is a shadow, and very shrewd about his identity."

"That's not good, but it certainly tells me I am dealing with a professional. How is the drug surveillance going on the bar?"

"Sorry. As you know, I am shut out of that investigation on a need to know basis."

"Alright. Well, thanks for your help, Lieutenant."

CHAPTER THIRTY-SEVEN

Roy Dwyer → Roid Wire with Leslie

After Lt. Mehle's uninformative telephone call, I went to the gym. My place for relaxation and meditation. I could clear my mind and dwell on other things. My gym had the usual collection running from plump women to bulky musclebound body builders and everything in between. I was happy to see all of them engaged in physical exercise. Especially the plump women and the older folks—they were active and interested in improving themselves. It didn't matter whether they were world champions or just trying to be healthy, they were active. Even the huge weightlifters were welcome—to lift heavy weights or develop a muscular physique generally required a devotion over a long term, and a disciplined regiment of at least three times a week. These hunks although scary looking were usually gentle and shy.

For me, it was peace. Cares melted away and new ideas f lowed as my body got tired and my mind was freed of obstructions. However, today the name "Roy Dwyer" kept coming up as I did my reps and counted. "Roy Dwyer, Roy Dwyer…" The names started to run together as "Roydwyer." I found myself staring off into space and taking in a conversation between two people at the next machine. As happens in the gym, the conversation was about anabolic steroids as the two people were speculating about one of the immense body builders' usage of performance enhancing drugs. The word "roid" popped up as I was counting my reps. Then, it hit me. "Roid Wire." Could this Roy Dwyer have some illegal drug connection to an illegal internet source for steroids known as the "Roid Wire." I did not want to ask one of the immense beasts there and then in my gym—they might be insulted, or afraid of a drug bust. So I called an old friend who had been a "professional body builder." That meant he competed in meets because everyone he was competing against was on the juice, like him.

"So, Bruce, David Magen here. I'm doing an investigation and came across the name 'Roid Wire.' Does it mean anything to you?" "Dave. Good to hear from you. Yeah. 'Roid Wire,' it was a source where you could get Mexican juice and pills, but it was shut down. Some narcs were in the locker rooms and squeezed a few guys till they gave up their source. What's up?"

"I think I found the old owner of the website."

That evening, I called my daughter—a savvy expert on all things computer. I had tried all versions I could think of for 'Roid Wire' on my computer, but my daughter was always a big help. My generation was way behind hers in all IT.

"Sweet pea. I'm doing some research on some druggies and a name came up which was supposed to be an outlet for steroids known as 'Roid Wire.' I tried a few passes at it on the internet but got nowhere. It may have been shut down some years ago. Do you think you could find it?"

"Sure, Dad. I'll try. If it wasn't taken down, but was simply not used, it's still there somewhere."

The next day, Leslie a.k.a. "Sweet Pea" buzzed in. "Dad, I think I've found it. There's an old defunct website under the name 'Roid Wire.' It's at least five years out of existence but was never shut down. It looks like a site selling steroids out of a New Jersey post office address. The phone number is dead, and the website manager doesn't know anything. It looks like a dead end."

"Okay, thanks, Sweet Pea. This guy is pretty good about covering his tracks. Thanks anyway."

CHAPTER THIRTY-EIGHT

Settlement on Bar, to Mehle

This Roy Dwyer gave me a call to set up the settlement on the bar, real estate, liquor license, etc. He emailed me the documents he wanted signed. The name of the buyer was blank in all, as I suspected. I forwarded them to Peter Lynch for his secretary to sign. I then took a bit of a risk. I prepared a release for the new buyer to sign along with Roy Dwyer. In it I put a complete restitution of the facts about the bar—the title ownership of the bar by Lynch's secretary but the averment that the true owner was Juan Diaz, who had died. That the proceeds would be held in escrow pending a claim by the heir of Diaz. That there had been an arrest for prostitution and drugs at the bar which might cause the real estate or the liquor license to be forfeited to the state. I had the buyer acknowledge all of this, and accept the transaction with full disclosure. Someday, the owner of the real estate and liquor license would be known because both documents would become public records, so I expected to see someone purporting to be the owner at settlement. It would be unnecessary to conceal someone whose identity would become known in a matter of days.

Then, I had an idea. I expected to have at least three people representing the buyer at the settlement—Roy Dwyer, the buyer's lawyer and the alleged buyer. I still needed to find out who this Roy Dwyer was, and hoped I could collect some DNA or fingerprints from the paper or a water glass. But then, I thought to bring Carmen along as my summer intern paralegal in case she could identify anyone.

Settlement was scheduled at a beat up older storefront office on Castor Avenue in Northeast Philadelphia. The office furniture was old and cheap, the walls showed scuff marks from the chairs, and the carpet was low grade industrial. Lawyers are often the worst snobs and judge each other like dogs sniffing each others butts. Our clothes, our shoes, our cars, but most important our offices betrayed our social rank, and presumably the quality of our legal services. This judgment was, of course, entirely spurious. I knew many extremely competent lawyers who disdained the expenditures of unnecessary funds on oriental carpets, antiques, thick rugs, receptionists with pseudo-english accents. But this office was below shabby.

We were ushered into a beat up conference room and sat at someone's old dining room table. Roy and his lawyer were there along with the title clerk who would conduct the settlement. I shuffled the papers across the table which had already been executed by Margaret Mary O'Leary along with a Power of Attorney allowing me to sign any other documents we may have forgotten as her legal stand-in. We also gave him a Management Contract permitting the buyer to operate the bar in the meantime pending approval of the LCB. So far, no sign from Carmen who looked bored.

Opposing counsel had passed the bank check to the title clerk. Suddenly, Roy tapped the attorney on the shoulder and they got up to leave the room. When they returned, they wanted a Release from Peter Lynch as to all these documents and a further agreement to execute any documents needed to complete the transaction to divest himself of any interest he had in the bar and real estate. I agreed to do this, but since Peter was not there, we would have to postpone settlement. They said they would prepare this document and scan it to him if his secretary would verify his signature. While we were doing this, the alleged buyer came in.

The lawyer struggled through a half-assed Release and Quit Claim for Peter Lynch to sign. As he came back into the room with typed copies for my review, three men walked into the room with him. These must be the buyer and his posse. I had already alerted Peter to the new document request and he had agreed it would not be a problem.

As we were sending off the document to Peter, Carmen followed me into the office and was clinging to my side and looking at me with imploring eyes. I motioned to her to keep quiet as the scanner was emailing the document.

She motioned me to the front of the storefront. "Alright, Carmen. What's up?"

"First I got one of that Roy Dwyer's cigarettes out of the ashtray while you were out."

"Wow, where is it?"

"In a gum wrapper in my purse."

"Whoa! Brilliant! Carmen you are a gem!"

"Wait, I'm not done. I recognize one of the men and I think he recognizes me."

"How do you know them?"

"The one guy—the white guy—is the other cop." "No shit. Are you sure?"

"Yeah. Not the one that arrested me, but the other one." "The AG cop."

"Yeah. That one."

"That's major. Now stay calm and let me get you out of here in one piece." We went back in. I don't know about Carmen, but my heart was beating a mile a minute. We had at the table no more than three feet away—the conspirators of the plot—the cop who orchestrated the raid, whose name was being concealed from us, and his accomplice of some kind—Roy Dwyer, the very professional possible owner of the "Roid Wire" website who was so adept at concealing his identity and two others. But I had to stay calm. Carmen and I came back into the conference room. Carmen was cool as a cucumber and started to assemble our copies of the signed documents and paperclip them. The buyer it turned out was the surly bartender I had handed my business card to earlier. He spoke with a heavy Spanish accent and had not lost a whit of his surliness. He was bored and went to his phone to surf a few apps. The other man who accompanied him did the same. Eventually, the email of the signed Release and Quit Claim came back from Peter Lynch. After a few more calculations, the title clerk began to sign checks. After a few deductions for water and sewer, real estate taxes, and a few minor items, the clerk handed me a check payable to Margaret Mary O'Leary for about $148,000. Trying not to let my hand shake, I put the check in my file and left with Carmen. She had earned an immense meal and I did not want to be followed. I deposited the check into the Lynch law firm escrow account at its branch on Castor Ave and weaved through the city to the Mt. Airy Diner. I sat with the car facing the street to see if anyone had followed us. Then I parked my beautiful 2002 metallic red Thunderbird behind the diner. I called Lt. Mehle on my cell phone.

"Lt. Mehle, David Magen here. I've got some big news. I'm a bit afraid of some of the evidence we stirred up so I want you to record this call in case anything happens to us."

"Who is us?"

"Carmen Jacinto and I."

"Okay, you're on speaker and on record. What have you got?"

"I was acting as Peter Lynch's lawyer selling the real estate liquor license etc. to this Roy Dwyer I told you about earlier. On a hunch, I brought Carmen along pretending to be a summer intern paralegal. First, she got a cigarette butt of this Dwyer which we need you to analyze for fingerprints or DNA.

"Next and even better, she can identify the second cop at her arrest. He is associated with and may even be the buyer. The bartender claimed to be the buyer, but it looked like this cop was the one in charge along with Roy Dwyer. Carmen can identify him she says. So we need a photo array of LCB or AG cops from the area. He is a tall white guy, no Spanish accent, in his forties, with salt and pepper hair. He may have a reddish tattoo on the inside of his left forearm."

"Thanks, Mr. Magen. Now we may have more than one dirty cop so I'm back in business. I want you and Carmen in here late this afternoon."

"Three okay?" "Fine."

Carmen had been listening. "What do I do with this cigarette butt?" "You keep it and give it to Lt. Mehle."

"Now do we eat?"

"Yes Carmen, we eat now."

Although it was lunchtime, Carmen had the entire turkey platter with stuffing and two sides, cranberry sauce, a coffee milkshake and two pieces of peach cobbler followed by a large coke. I could only look on humbly over my chef salad with oil and vinegar and a coke zero; but my diet was intact.

CHAPTER THIRTY-NINE

Carmen with Mehle ID's AG Cop

Once Carmen said she could identify the second policeman at the settlement and thought he could recognize her, I knew we could be in danger. Carmen gave me the name of another family in New Jersey where she could stay until summer school started so I deposited her with them and told them to maintain strict silence on Carmen's whereabouts. I picked her up the next day and brought her to Mehle's office for her interview.

As we walked into IAD headquarters and were ushered into its barebones conference room, I was happy to see Lt. Mehle had been joined by the IAD Inspector Harvey McAllister—a large black man with tons of experience in many divisions of the police department, and a man of unquestioned integrity. He was also a part time preacher at a large black church. When he spoke, his deep bass voice could cause the venetian blinds to rattle. We had now gotten the attention of the senior brass and were believed.

After appropriate introductions and an update on the status of the case to date for Inspector McAllister, Lt. Mehle began to call up personnel pictures from files of the Attorney General's police staff. He had eliminated everyone who would not be called a tall white male. Carmen identified no one.

We then went to the files of the state police assigned to the Liquor Control Board. The third picture was Edward Reynolds and Carmen nailed him. No doubt. Sure enough, he was 6'2" and had once been with the Attorney General's office, but had transferred a few years earlier. He was a weight lifter and had an imposing physique. There had been an administrative inquiry about ten years earlier as to some of his past activities, but he had been cleared.

On a hunch, I asked if we could review some of the personnel photos to see if Roy Dwyer might show up. I had them adjust for his height (about 5'6"), his age (over fifty) and include some retired members of the state police and the Attorney General's office. Sure enough, Roy Dwyer showed up as Joseph Lascone. He had been retired about ten years and had been involved in the same inquiry as Edward Reynolds. His retirement had occurred in the same year when the inquiry had taken place. There was a file number attached to the inquiry but the file was marked for restricted access. Fortunately, the IAD police could easily get through these restricted access blocks on files.

Lt. Mehle told us to go out for an hour for a snack while he researched the file. He had the look of an energized bloodhound who could smell a good trail.

We left and went to a local DQ. That day they were having a two for one deal on a Blizzard—some kind of ice cream concoction with added f lavors, jimmies, sprinkles, M&Ms. I don't need to say that I had neither of the two Blizzards—you probably know who did. I had a sugar free popsicle which was very good, thank you.

When we returned, Lt. Mehle and Inspector McAllister were all smiles. Our "Roy Dwyer" and Edward Reynolds had been ratted out by some other cops who were also body builders. The two cops both were working for the Allentown police department and were allegedly selling anabolic steroids at gyms in the area. Somehow, the investigations got botched up and Joseph Lascone aka "Roy Dwyer" had been permitted to retire with a full pension. Edward Reynolds transferred a year later to the Attorney General's office. His attorney at the time was a former Attorney General who was later disbarred for receiving kickbacks from illegal poker machine operators. The steroid sales were apparently made when Reynolds or Lascone handed out cards for the Roy Dwyer email site. The buyers could then access the site with a code number and have their parcels of pills or injectables sent to their designated addresses by regular mail.

Lt. Mehle then had Carmen escorted back to her summer school after making arrangements for the nuns to take care of her until the other girls showed up at the dorm. As it happened there was a ballet summer camp on site and she was in a dorm with the dancers.

Meanwhile, the $148,000 check was safely in the bank and I had no further need to contact "Roy Dwyer," and legally I owed him nothing if he subsequently lost the bar. I had warned him and Joseph Lascone in advance, disclosed the shaky status of the title and gotten a release. I hadn't promised not to rat them out. I called Peter Lynch to warn him and gave a full briefing on what had transpired.

CHAPTER FORTY

McCready Call

Without any prior notice, I got a call from Sgt. McCready. He had been very uncooperative before and I couldn't believe he wanted to cooperate now.

"Mr. Magen. Glad I could reach you. We've had a few things turn up in the investigation and I wanted to ask you a few questions."

"I offered my help before and you weren't interested. What inspired this joyous turn of events?"

"Oh yeah, sorry about that. We've been interviewing Emilio about the hit on Diaz. He claims you were in on it and wanted to take over the bar for your client Peter Lynch. Could this be true?"

"You actually gave this tale some credibility? First, I have no interest in the bar, nor does Peter Lynch. He makes a decent living and has no interest in owning and operating a drug bar, much less putting out a hit on his own client to take it over. Why would you think such a thing? What else does Emilio say?"

"He was offered a 50% interest in the bar but he needed to know who was threatening his old boss—Luis Diaz. He was told you know who this is and, if he got you to talk, you could tell him."

"That's a crock. Does he say who made him this offer? I never knew then who was threatening this Luis Diaz."

"Maybe, your client Carmen did?" "No way."

"So he attacked me to get information I didn't have?"

"He really wanted to get to Carmen but was told she was put in protective custody."

"When he attacked me, neither Carmen or I knew who this other person was."

"I'm sensing you know something, but you're not telling me." "First, I don't know you, I don't like you and I don't trust you. You haven't done some of the obvious things in this investigation and I don't know why. You haven't given me some information I need so why should I help you?"

"You could be obstructing justice." Now he was getting nasty. My disclosure to Mehle and McAllister was complete and honest and saved me from any withholding evidence issue. I wasn't going to help this guy McCready if I didn't have to. Payback's a bitch as they say.

"I'll certainly mention that at your administrative hearing." "Okay, okay. I get it. What do you want to know?"

"First, why haven't you had the bar under surveillance? Obviously, there is still drug traffic going on. Obviously, the one who is conducting the traffic is the murderer. I know it is not Peter Lynch. If you could identify who was supplying the bar with drugs, I think you could nail a big supplier."

"How do you know drugs are being sold at the bar?" "I went there and saw it. Why didn't you?"

"The narcotics unit has taken over that part of the investigation." "Aha! And they claim they have surveilled the bar and found nothing."

"As far as I know."

"Did Emilio tell you he knew who was the one that threatened the bar owner? He was the bartender who sold the drugs and received the delivery from Luis Diaz. If the bar changed hands, he might have been in contact with the guy who wanted to take over the bar."

"Emilio says no. He's mad because he lost his cushy job."

"Even though he is facing major prison time for assaulting me and selling drugs as well as fostering prostitution, he has nothing to say to save him from some prison time?"

"So far."

"To be fair, I sense an incompetent investigation that is not exploiting its leads and an arrogant cop who thinks he's right. I have no faith in the security of your investigation so I'm going elsewhere. Grab your ankles!"

As McCready was starting to blurble something into the phone, I hung up. I had made the right choice going through Mehle. I knew he would maintain security during his investigation and he would be absolutely straight. I didn't trust McCready—he was either incompetent or corrupt. My information might find its way to Lascone or Roy Dwyer to disasterous effects—loss of evidence, shaky witnesses and just plain dumb policework.

CHAPTER FORTY-ONE

To Mehle—The Feds

When I spoke to Mehle, he had wisely brought in the feds. The DEA had power, money, men, credibility and maintained a healthy suspicion of local cops—especially narcs. But best of all were the federal agents and federal sentences. The DEA could afford to build a case slowly and completely, without any holes. They could try cases from the city of Philadelphia in federal court where they could depend on decent judges and whitebread suburban jurors to trust in good policework and not get bamboozled by an obfuscatory defense lawyer.

As we spoke, the feds of course had already surveilled the bar, bugged the area where the drugs were sold and logged hundreds of hours taping those coming and going to the bar—especially those carrying packages. They scared the crap out of Emilio who started to sing like a nightingale. He described an offer from Luis Diaz' partner—previously unknown—to let him have a 25% interest in the bar if he could "neutralize" whoever killed Luis. The offer was through a third person. With that much money on the line, he thought Peter Lynch was the one who killed Diaz and that Carmen was the witness who could kill the deal. I was collateral damage to get to Carmen. He didn't remember me from my visit to the bar but thought I would give up Carmen's whereabouts.

Cocaine was purchased by the feds several times at the bar, and tested and sealed in plastic. The entire transactions were recorded on cameras pinned on the fed informants. Once the amount purchased equaled a sufficient weight for a large sentence, Reynolds and Lascone were brought in.

In federal court, the length of your sentence depends on the provable amount of drugs the feds can claim were sold. When combined with a murder charge, police corruption and conspiracy, they were looking at a jail term longer than the life of the Roman Empire. While they were lawyering up, their underlings were more than happy to flip on them because the case against them was so solid. The sentences are pretty much fixed by the "Sentencing Guidelines" which require federal judges to award terms of incarceration at least three times that of state court or write a long opinion as to why they were more lenient. The judges were of course intimidated that their opinions might make them sound like wimps.

The only game in town was to "cooperate," that is to provide useful information against someone else. This usually cut their sentences in half and avoided the "Sentencing Guide" ranges.

With some high priced lawyers eager to earn a fee, Reynolds and Lascone held out. They thought the "underlings" who ratted them out would not be credible against two cops who had done well to insulate them from the bar operation. Besides it was an all or nothing proposition. They were looking at two life sentences plus plus plus if they were found guilty and enough time to make them old men or die in prison if they plead guilty.

As the feds supplied their lawyers with more and more evidence that they were guilty, Lascone and Reynolds began to waver but not fold. Their underlings all said they owned the bar and supplied the drugs, but it was their word alone. No one yet could put them at the bar. My testimony identified Roy Dwyer as paying me $2000 and representing a person buying the bar. Lascone was only present at the settlement. The feds dug into the "Roid Wire" sale of steroids and started interviewing the investigators who allowed the case to slip between the cracks and go unprosecuted. Although the statute of limitations was long passed in this case, it could be used as evidence in the current case.

Lascone and Reynolds still refused to budge.

CHAPTER FORTY-TWO

Before actually arresting Dwyer and Lascone, the feds wanted to get a search warrant and raid the bar. At 8:00PM about twenty FBI and DEA agents raided the bar. The new beer box full of coke and meth had arrived about 6:00PM and would be nearly full. The messenger delivering the box had also been stopped and searched. He had $26,000 in cash on him. He was locked up and his car was forfeited. There was nearly a kilogram of coke and meth at the bar as well as $4,000.

However, the most interesting thing about the raid was that the coke and meth were already bagged in sales portions and each bag was stamped with the particular brand name of the dealer. The names on the bags, however, were all from dealers in the Coatesville area— about 40 miles away from Tito's way past the far western suburbs. The brands were not all from the same drug dealer but from four different street dealers. This was a huge irregularity. These dealers were all rivals and would shoot each other on sight. How did their stuff end up commingled in a beer box in Tito's in the lower northeast of Philadelphia? The AG agents were selling it to Lascone and Dwyer for resale at the bar.

The FBI ordered immediate fingerprint tests of the goods. Ah, the FBI lab —quick, efficient and accurate. The results were back in a few hours. The fingerprints on the bags were a few street dealers from Coatesville and some AG agents. Some cops had touched these bags after an arrest was made, and before the beer box was delivered to Tito's.

Within hours, the computers had spit out arrests where the AG agents had made arrests of the street dealers whose brands appeared on the bags in Tito's beer box. The next day, DEA agents fanned out to interview the street dealers whose brands were in the box about their recent arrests. To a man, they were able to state that the amount of drugs in the arrest was understated and the AG agents had kept a large portion of the drugs. The dealers were happy not to report the discrepancy because their punishment was lessened if the weight of their drugs were lessened. Since they were now given immunity and a "deal," they were happy to tell the truth.

It was now time to interview the agents. It turned out that there were three. They were offered a "deal," if they could say who they sold the drugs to. Of course, they were fired as cops but their prison sentences would be five years instead of fifteen. Each man implicated Lascone and one implicated "Roy Dwyer."

Reynolds aka Dwyer and Lascone were brought in and shown tapes of the AG agents ratting them out, as well as the street dealers ratting the AG agents out.

Lt. Mehle had hit a home run. He had broken out a chain of dirty cops with good police work. Now, Lascone and Dwyer were looking at enough years in jail so they would never see the streets again, even without the murder rap. They still would not plea; but the trial on everything but the murder was a foregone conclusion now. The feds elected to try all the drug police corruption, conspiracy cases first in one trial. They would introduce evidence of the murder, but hold the actual murder trial for last.

Huge headlines broke the story, locally and nationally.

Needless to say the bar and real estate were forfeited. The Philadelphia cops who cooperated with Lascone and Dwyer in the first raid were investigated and fired.

Carmen's name was never in the print or TV media. Only "Flora" was named. Bastoncino was called in on a confidential Disciplinary Board Hearing and quietly relieved of his license to practice law.

Several months after all the dust cleared, I got a call from Lt. Mehle. He wanted Carmen and me to come to his office. It was late summer, Carmen had completed her remedial summer school and had been accepted full time at the Catholic boarding school.

When we got to the IAD office, we were ushered into the same conference room. This time, the Lynches and the Police Commissioner were there, and looked to be happy and smiling.

First, the police commissioner spoke: "Carmen, we want to thank you for being such a standup person in this investigation. After all, you identified for me Judge Bastoncino and former Lt. Lascone. Your school tells us you are doing well. We cannot recognize you officially in the media, but we wanted to give you this commendation for your service and wish you well."

Then, Liam Lynch stood up. "Carmen, we hear from Mr. Magen, that you had no Quinceañera when you were fifteen. So we have arranged a special graduation party for when you graduate high school at a fancy hotel downtown. You are a junior now, but at the end of your senior year you will have a special bash downtown."

Carmen, of course was completely surprised. I could see her little lip start to quiver and she buried her face in my jacket and cried.

Bio

Richard Malmed has been a trial lawyer in Philadelphia for 48 years. Before that, he had been an English Literature major at Yale University. Now in semi-retirement, he has been busting to write a few novels combining cases he has handled over the years.